PAUL GREEN

THERE COMES AN EVIL DAY

Complete and Unabridged

LINFORD
Leicester

First published in Great Britain in 2013 by
Robert Hale Limited
London

First Linford Edition
published 2015
by arrangement with
Robert Hale Limited
London

A catalogue record for this book is available from the British Library.

ISBN 978–1–4448–2392–9

Published by
F. A. Thorpe (Publishing)
Anstey, Leicestershire

Set by Words & Graphics Ltd.
Anstey, Leicestershire
Printed and bound in Great Britain by
T. J. International Ltd., Padstow, Cornwall

This book is printed on acid-free paper

7000000254462

SPECIAL MESSAGE TO READERS

THE ULVERSCROFT FOUNDATION
(registered UK charity number 264873)

was established in 1972 to provide funds for research, diagnosis and treatment of eye diseases. Examples of major projects funded by the Ulverscroft Foundation are:-

- The Children's Eye Unit at Moorfields Eye Hospital, London
- The Ulverscroft Children's Eye Unit at Great Ormond Street Hospital for Sick Children
- Funding research into eye diseases and treatment at the Department of Ophthalmology, University of Leicester
- The Ulverscroft Vision Research Group, Institute of Child Health
- Twin operating theatres at the Western Ophthalmic Hospital, London
- The Chair of Ophthalmology at the Royal Australian College of Ophthalmologists

You can help further the work of the Foundation by making a donation or leaving a legacy. Every contribution is gratefully received. If you would like to help support the Foundation or require further information, please contact:

THE ULVERSCROFT FOUNDATION
The Green, Bradgate Road, Anstey
Leicester LE7 7FU, England
Tel: (0116) 236 4325

website: www.foundation.ulverscroft.com

THERE COMES AN EVIL DAY

Fugitive bank robber George Munro's dramatic escape from Yuma Prison was taken as a personal affront by his captor, Marshal Sean Barry. Having finally tracked his quarry down to the sleepy border town of San Tomas, Sean is disappointed to find only a grave — and the dead man's twin brother, a crusading priest. Father Joseph Munro is determined to rid San Tomas of the ex-Confederate marauders, led by the ruthless Colonel Silas Quinn, who brutally control the town. Can Sean help the cleric win his fight?

Books by Paul Green
in the Linford Western Library:

THE DEVIL'S PAYROLL
LAST DAY IN PARADISE

1

Marshal Sean Barry emerged out of a sandstorm that had been blowing for hours across the Chihuahua desert. He slowed his horse to a halt and raised a gloved hand to shield his eyes from the grit which blew relentlessly into his face. He was almost blinded by the swirling clouds of dust and could barely make out the name of this small town, *San Tomas*, carved on a battered wooden sign by the roadside near the Mexican border. It was a long way from Yuma Prison but it was here that Sean hoped to find the man he had been hunting for almost two years: George Munro.

Munro's daring escape had made headline news and for six months following it, Sean had chased rumours of his presence in various towns throughout Texas. Then, the trail had suddenly gone cold and he reluctantly turned his attention to the various other outlaws who required bringing to justice. Nevertheless, Munro's evasion of a twenty-year sentence irked him considerably. When he had received an anonymous note just two weeks ago, informing him that the man he was looking for was to be found in this sleepy border town, he had no hesitation in following it up. It was Sean himself who had originally hunted down and captured Munro following a failed bank robbery and he took the man's escape almost as a personal affront. The law was there to be obeyed and those who failed to heed it did so at their peril. If Munro really was in San Tomas, he was about to discover that he could no longer flout the law with impunity. Dead or alive, Sean was going to bring him in.

As he rode past the rows of adobe and sandstone buildings, the tolling of a bell sounded faintly above the howling wind and he made out the shape of a church tower at the other end of the town. Sean recalled that it was Sunday and many of the inhabitants would be in church. He knew little about the place, other than that it had been Mexican territory before the State of Texas was founded and was populated by a mixture of Hispanic and white Americans, the majority of whom were Catholics. Thus the town had retained the name of the famous doubting apostle after becoming part of Texas more than thirty years before. Sean had little time for religion himself, having seen too much of men's wickedness, and the scepticism reputedly shown by the saint suited him just fine. He had no real evidence that Munro was really hiding in this backwater and would not believe it until he saw him up close.

The storm was dying away now and Sean pulled the bandanna down from over his nose and mouth. Munro would certainly not be in church, he knew that much, and the main street was deserted. As he rode further on, he heard the sound of a tinkling piano, accompanied by raucous laughter. The noises were coming from a gaudily painted clapboard building to his right. A sign above the batwings informed him that it was The Bad Angel, a hotel, saloon and gaming house with a livery next door. Sean was about to dismount and go inside but then decided to report to the sheriff first. The jailhouse was a few doors down but the building was closed, with no sign of anyone inside when he peered through the grimy window. Still, it was Sunday after all and even sheriffs were entitled to a day of rest.

Sean tethered his horse and entered the saloon. All eyes turned towards the tall man shaking the dust from his long coat as he stepped across the threshold. A single streak of white was visible in the shock of jet-black hair which appeared when he removed his hat. A pair of bright emerald eyes deep set above an unshaven chin swept the room. Seeing no sign of his quarry, Sean stepped up to the bar.

'I'll have a cold beer, please,' he announced, tossing a silver dollar down in front of the gaunt individual who stood wiping a glass.

'Sure,' replied the bartender, as he poured the drink. Then his eyes widened in surprise when Sean removed his dustcoat to reveal a silver star pinned to his jacket.

'We don't get many lawmen in these parts,' the man said, clearing his throat nervously.

Sean slid the faded wanted poster he carried with him across the bar between them. 'I'm looking for this man. Have you seen him?' he asked.

'Well I'll be damned!' exclaimed the bartender as he stared at the poster. 'He's even got the same surname too, but it can't be him, surely!'

'What do you mean?' demanded Sean.

'The outlaw in that there picture is a dead ringer for the priest here, Fr Munro.'

Sean shook his head. 'It wouldn't be the first time an outlaw's disguised himself as some kind of preacher. Maybe I ought to go up to that church and take a look myself.'

The bartender's bird-like features twisted into a frown. 'No, that can't be it. Father Munro's been here ten years at least and never been away from the place. It says on this here poster that your man escaped from Yuma two years back.'

'Let me take a look at that.' The words came from a burly, red-bearded individual dressed in a faded grey tunic with three yellow stripes on the arm, obviously a veteran of the Confederate Army. The bartender licked his narrow lips nervously and handed over the poster, his hand trembling.

The former sergeant removed a pipe from his mouth and let out a deep, throaty chuckle. 'Yeah, it sure does look like him, don't it?'

'Then I guess I'll go see for myself,' said Sean.

The man looked up at him and tapped the cheap tin star pinned to his tunic. 'I'm Deputy Sheriff Al Drake. You see, I'm a lawman too.'

'What of it?'

Drake grinned, showing a row of broken teeth. 'It means I can say who goes pokin' around this place and who don't.'

'I'm Marshal Sean Barry and I have a warrant for Munro's arrest,' replied Sean. 'That entitles me to search this town for him, whether you like it or not.'

Drake's piggy little eyes blazed with fury. 'Now look here, Marshal. That priest ain't nothin' but a heap o' trouble but you don't bother nobody in San Tomas without my say so. Now, ask real nice and I might just let you wander on up to that church. If not, you can just skedaddle on outa here.'

'You said you were the deputy sheriff. How about letting me ask the real boss, not his pet monkey?'

By the time Drake's hand had reached his holster, Sean was already pressing the muzzle of his own weapon into the former sergeant's fat belly. Drake raised his hands reluctantly as the marshal stepped back towards the door.

'You're makin' a big mistake. Colonel Quinn won't like this one bit.'

'On the contrary, Drake, I rather enjoyed seeing you squirm for a change.'

Both men looked up as the man who had spoken descended a flight of stairs towards them. He was impeccably groomed from the polished boots to the gleaming gold thread on the epaulettes of his grey uniform.

'I am Colonel Silas Quinn, Marshal. Do please forgive my deputy's excessive show of enthusiasm for enjoying the privileges of his office.' He dismissed Drake with a wave of his gloved hand and then smoothed down a mane of fair hair as he removed a plumed hat. It matched his crisply curling beard, lending the officer a rather leonine appearance.

Sean put his pistol back into its

holster. ‘You ought to choose your men more carefully, Colonel, or should I address you as Sheriff?’

Quinn flashed him a smile and spread his hands expansively. ‘Either will do, Marshal, but really, I must perform my humble duties as best I can with the men the Lord gave me. We’re all only made from clay after all.’

‘Then I guess by the look of things the soil around here isn’t too good.’

‘In that case may I suggest you get on with your search, Marshal? Then you can find some place in which the soil is more to your liking.’ Quinn’s smile remained fixed but there was now an edge to the polite southern drawl. Sean’s instincts told him that beneath the elegant manners, the officer-turned-sheriff was not a man to be trifled with. He gave him a curt nod and then headed out through the doors back into the glare of sunlight.

When he had gone, Drake sidled up to his boss like a whipped dog. ‘Shall I put a bullet in his back, sir?’

Quinn looked at him with contempt. 'No, you fool. We don't want some other lawman turning up here to find out what happened to him. Just follow at a distance but stay out of sight. Do you think you can manage that?'

Drake nodded enthusiastically and crept out of the saloon. Ahead of him, Sean was striding towards the white-washed church. Above the doorway there was a wooden statue of an astonished Thomas kneeling before the risen Christ. He glanced up at it and stepped inside into the candlelit gloom, remembering to remove his hat as he did so. The service was almost over and Sean withdrew into a side chapel as the congregation filed out past him. The priest remained kneeling in front of the altar, his head bowed in prayer.

Sean marched up purposefully towards the bent figure. If the priest heard his approach, he showed no sign of it and remained where he was. As he drew nearer, the marshal began to feel nervous. If this really was an innocent cleric, he did not want to make a complete fool of himself. He stopped a few feet from the kneeling figure and cleared his throat nervously.

The priest straightened his back, made the sign of the cross and then stood before turning to face him. Sean's jaw dropped and he reached for his gun. He really was staring into the craggy, bearded features and pale-blue eyes of George Munro.

'You can stop pretending, Munro. I'm taking you in.'

'I take it you're Marshal Sean Barry, looking for George Munro?'

Sean prodded him with his revolver. 'Skip it, you know darn well who I am and that it's you I've come for.'

The priest shook his head gently. 'I am Joseph Munro and I have not left this town once in the past eleven years. George was my twin brother.'

'Tell that to the guards at Yuma Prison. Maybe they'll let you go.'

'Ask anyone in this town who I am and how long I've been here. You won't find a single person to say I'm not Father Joseph Munro.'

Sean hesitated, recalling what he had been told in the saloon. How could an escaped convict successfully pass himself off as a priest in the priest's own parish? Still, he could not deny the evidence of his own eyes. Surely even identical twins differed slightly in appearance?

'Even our own mother couldn't tell us apart,' said Munro, as if reading his thoughts.

'Somebody sent me a note, telling me that George was here.'

Munro smiled in response. 'Come, I'll show you.' Then he turned and walked through the sacristy before opening a door that led to a cemetery behind the church. Sean followed closely behind, his pistol aimed at the priest's back. Munro stopped in front of a plain wooden cross in a secluded corner of the churchyard which had the name *George Munro* carved on it. The grave had been neatly tended and was decorated with fresh flowers.

Sean shrugged. 'That doesn't prove anything.'

The priest nodded. 'You're right. You could dig up my brother's skeleton if you wanted and that wouldn't prove it was him either but I can explain everything if you're prepared to listen.'

Sean put his gun back in its holster. 'I'm all ears.'

'George arrived here about eighteen months ago, late at night. He was on the run and sick with fever. I took him in and tended him as best I could, but he died after a few days. I didn't tell anyone he was here and buried him myself, tucked out of the way where the grave wouldn't be noticed.'

'Someone must have noticed,' Sean pointed out. 'I received a note telling me I'd find him here.'

Munro nodded. 'Yes, I sent it to you.'

'Do you mean to say that you dragged me all this way across the desert just to show me your brother's grave?'

The priest responded calmly to

Sean's blast of rage. 'No, Marshal, I brought you here to uphold the law and defend the people of this town against their enemies.'

'That's why people elect a sheriff, isn't it?'

'Have you met Quinn and that oaf, Drake?'

Sean nodded. 'Yeah, I met them. They're hardly the sort of men I'd choose, but it's not my business.'

Munro stepped closer to him. 'Let me tell you about Quinn and his followers. There's a whole gang of them, ex-Confederates who went to Mexico to fight for the Emperor Maximilian. They were given money and land but lost it all when the revolutionaries won and kicked them out. Quinn brought his men here about a year ago. They started shooting up the town, killed the sheriff, his deputy and anyone else who tried to stand up to them.'

'Are you telling me that Quinn controls San Tomas, that he appointed himself sheriff?'

The priest nodded wearily. 'It's worse than that, I'm afraid. He and his men extort money and goods from all the businesses in the town. They live free at the hotel and drink as much as they like. Anyone who opposes them is beaten and locked up in jail.'

'I don't know why you sent for me. You need the army here to restore order.'

Munro's face darkened. 'Do you imagine we haven't thought of that? When a man leaves town for any reason, two of Quinn's men go with him. If he tries to alert anyone, he's shot. The same applies if he tries to escape. Besides, we're miles from the nearest fort.'

'Can't someone sneak out, at night for example?'

Munro shook his head. 'Quinn has men posted on top of a canyon just outside the town. Anyone entering or leaving is soon spotted — '

A faint rustling sound caused Sean to raise his hand, silencing the priest. Then he turned, gun in hand, to see a stout figure scurrying away from the edge of the cemetery. He wondered how long Drake had been watching them.

'He'll tell Quinn we've been talking and you'll be followed if you leave San Tomas,' Munro told him. 'They'll hunt you down like a dog before you reach the nearest town.'

'Then why the hell did you bring me here, damn it? Just what do you expect me to do?' Sean demanded angrily.

'The people here are scared and they need someone to lead them, someone who won't be afraid to stand up to Quinn and his men. Perhaps then they can find the courage within themselves to rid San Tomas of this wickedness.'

'Why me, Father? I just bring in the men I'm told to. I do the job I'm paid for, that's all and I wasn't ordered to clean up this town by any judge.'

Munro seized his arm and spoke more urgently. 'Don't wait to be told what to do: listen to your conscience!' Then he stepped back and fixed Sean with a hard look of appraisal. 'When my brother lay dying, he feared you coming after him more than any bounty hunter or posse. I learned of how you first captured him, how you killed the other five members of his gang in a gunfight before bringing him in for trial. If you uphold the law only when you are paid to do it, then you are no better than Quinn and his followers.'

'I guess you're right, Father, but this is a job for more than one man.'

'Sometimes one is all that is needed. Besides, there comes an evil day in every man's life when he is confronted with the utmost wickedness and must decide whether he will stand against it, alone if need be.'

'What about you, Father, what will you do?'

'As a priest I can't take up violence, but every Sunday I preach against what Quinn and his men are doing to this town. I can also offer you shelter in my home.'

Sean shook his head. 'No, if I'm

going to do this I must confront these men on their own ground. I'll stay in the hotel.'

'Then may God go with you.' Munro raised his hand in a gesture of blessing, then turned and walked back towards the church.

Sean took his horse to the livery and ordered the stable hand to give the animal a rub down, a good feed and plenty of water. Then he strode through the doors of the saloon once more and walked up to the gaunt bartender.

'I think I'll stick around here for a few days. Give me your best room.'

The man swallowed hard. 'Sheriff Quinn has the best room, sir.'

'Well, who has the second best one?'

'Oh, that belongs to his deputy.'

Sean grinned, spun the register towards him and crossed out Drake's name before writing his own in its place. 'There, that's settled. Now get me the key.'

The bartender licked his dry lips and his Adam's apple moved up and down as he swallowed hard.

'The room's already taken, mister.'

Sean turned around and saw a lean, straggly-haired young man standing before him. His grey tunic marked him out as one of Quinn's men and he had a red bandanna tied around his scrawny neck.

'I see, and who might you be?'

'I'm Luke Paterson.' He tapped the faded corporal's stripes on his arm. 'I can answer for Drake and he won't take this kindly. In fact you're just wastin' time 'cos all them rooms are taken. Ain't that right, Turner?'

The bartender nodded. 'That's right, Mr Paterson, all the rooms are taken.'

There was a tense silence, broken only by the ticking of a grandfather clock in a corner of the saloon. Card games came to a halt; every man set down his glass and the waitresses in their low-cut dresses stepped away from the customers they were serving or flirting with. All eyes were on Sean as people waited to see how he would respond.

'Why don't I fight Drake for that room?'

Paterson's eyes narrowed suspiciously. 'I hear you've outdrawn Drake once already so that ain't much of a contest, is it?'

'Oh I didn't mean with guns, just an old-fashioned street fight with fists.'

Paterson grinned as he looked over Sean's lean frame. 'Yeah, I like the odds on that one. Go call him, he's upstairs now.'

Sean went to the foot of the staircase which led to the hotel rooms and shouted, 'Hey, Drake! I want that room of yours so get your big fat ass down here! Do you hear me? Come down and fight me for it!'

Moments later, a dishevelled Drake came hurrying down the stairs, fastening his trousers as he did so. The woman behind him clutched a sheet around her ample breasts as she watched anxiously.

'Forget him, honey. You'll have a much better time with me!' Sean called to her.

The crowd in the saloon erupted into laughter and Drake was now flushed with rage as he lurched towards the object of his fury. Paterson stepped nimbly between them and whispered in the deputy sheriff's ear. Drake nodded and then looked up at Sean.

'If you knock me out you can have the room, but if I win you leave town. Is that it?'

Sean nodded as he moved towards the door. 'Come on, big man. I reckon you're just a heap of dough with a glass jaw.'

Drake grunted in response, his features twisted into a scowl. He had size and strength, but Sean suspected he was both dull witted and slow on his feet. Now he was angry and might make mistakes his opponent could exploit. A crowd spilled out on to the street to watch the fight as the two men circled each other. Quinn's men urged on their companion while the townspeople shouted words of encouragement to the marshal.

Sean clenched his fists into tight balls and prepared for an onslaught from his heavier opponent. If he won this fight, he might win over some support and put the first cracks in Quinn's sordid little empire. Should he lose, however, he might never leave San Tomas alive.

2

Drake made the first move, lurching towards Sean with a huge fist aimed squarely at his face. The marshal danced away on the balls of his feet, narrowly dodging the blow and then moved aside to avoid a second punch that would have winded an ox. Drake swore under his breath as Sean moved nimbly behind him. The larger man turned and was met with a punch under the jaw that sent him staggering. Sean moved in closer but Drake recovered before he could follow up with a second blow and the marshal found himself enveloped in a bear hug that squeezed the breath out of him. A fiery pain surged through his ribs as his burly opponent lifted him off his feet. Sean's arms were pinned to his sides and no amount of effort could free them. Then he looked into Drake's upturned face, contorted with effort and brought his head down in a crushing blow against his opponent's squat nose.

The deputy sheriff howled with pain, immediately letting go as his hands flew up to his face. Sean gasped for breath and rolled away as he was dropped to the ground but he was barely on his feet before Drake came lurching towards him, head down, with a bellow of rage. Sean was knocked backwards as the larger man cannoned into his chest like a charging bull. He hit the ground and then a huge fist reached out to grab him but he lashed out with a kick to Drake's knee that knocked his opponent off balance. Sean jumped to his feet and ploughed his fist into his adversary's stomach. Drake doubled up and the marshal followed with a blow under the chin that felled his opponent like a tree.

Sean stood panting for a moment as the larger man lay groaning in the dust. A cheer went up from the town's inhabitants and it looked as though the fight was over. There was a spring, with a statue of the Madonna, in the centre of the town and he went over to drink from it and to wash his face. He looked up, sensing a movement from behind before someone in the crowd shouted a warning. Then his head was forced under the water as Drake grabbed a fistful of hair and pressed down with all his might. Sean clawed desperately at the man's vice-like grip but it was to no avail. He had managed to draw in a deep breath before being ducked but was not sure how long he could hold it. There was only one thing he could do but it was a risky strategy.

Drake felt the marshal's body go limp as his opponent stopped struggling. He gave a grunt of satisfaction and then turned to face a jeering crowd, his own men the only ones who were applauding him. His eyes widened in disbelief when Sean spun him around and smashed a fist into his jaw. Now it was the marshal who was enraged, for nothing angered him more than a dirty fighter using underhand tactics. The advantage of surprise allowed him to land a series of blows to Drake's chest and face, pummelling the man's body mercilessly so that he staggered back, bloodied by the weight of Sean's onslaught. Finally, he slumped against a wagon and crumpled to the floor.

Drake's eyes were narrow slits in a bruised and swollen face. He fumbled in his pocket and tossed a room key down at Sean's feet, muttering that he had had enough. The marshal held it up for all to see and a great cheer went up as he walked back into the saloon. Paterson scowled and sent two of Quinn's men over to help the battered deputy sheriff to his feet.

'Your life won't be worth a dime when my boss hears about this,' muttered the ex-corporal as Sean walked passed him.

'I wouldn't be so sure of that. Quinn wants men who can fight, doesn't he?'

Silas Quinn stepped away from the window of his suite on the top floor. He had watched the fight carefully from his vantage point and was impressed by the marshal's cunning as well as his guts. A man like that could be a very dangerous enemy so perhaps it was time to turn him into a friend.

'This marshal has become something of a hero, no?' said Chiquita Sabatini as she stood beside him.

'Do you find him handsome, my dear?'

She fixed him with that mocking smile of hers. 'Of course, who would not?'

Quinn's eyes bore into her own and he placed his hands firmly on her shoulders. 'No one's going to take you away from me, my little songbird. Just remember who looks after you . . . and your father.'

The young woman shivered and her eyes were suddenly fearful. 'I know, Silas, I am grateful as always.'

'Good, now show me how grateful.'

Chiquita placed a hand on his cheek and drew his face towards hers, parting her lips to receive his hungry kiss. As she did so, however, it was an image of the young marshal that swam into her mind. If only he could be the one to save her.

Meanwhile, Sean eased his aching limbs into a tub and allowed himself a long soak. When he eventually got out, it felt good to put on fresh clothes and shave in front of the mirror in his spacious room. There was a knock at the door as he stood scraping the soap from his chin and then Silas Quinn entered, closing the door behind him.

'I thought it might be a good idea for us to talk.'

'Do you want me to beat up some of your other men for you?'

Quinn smiled. 'Drake's a fool but he has his uses. Brute strength gets rid of some opposition but you, on the other hand, have brains.'

Sean did not answer but continued shaving, then wiped his face with a towel. Quinn held up the deputy's badge Drake had been wearing.

'I've already got a badge, I don't need that one.'

'Whatever you're paid as a marshal, I'll double it,' said Quinn urgently.

'I know where the money comes from, Quinn, and I'm not interested in robbing people.'

Quinn laughed. 'I see — a man with scruples. I used to have those myself until I gave up on lost causes. Tell me, how many outlaws have you captured or killed?'

Sean shrugged. 'I stopped counting a long time ago. What's your point?'

The former colonel pulled up a chair and sat down. 'The world's still a pretty bad place and you're no better off. You can't do much to protect the weak, so, if you're strong, make the most of it, like I do.'

Sean looked at him with contempt. 'I'll never be like you, never. Now get out of here and leave me in peace.'

Quinn rose to his feet reluctantly. 'I'm disappointed in you, Mr Barry. You're obviously not as smart as I thought you were.' Then he paused in the doorway. 'I imagine that damn fool priest put you up to this, but you've no chance of winning, not against all my men put together.'

No, but I can pick you off gradually, Sean said to himself when Quinn had gone.

Al Drake was still very stiff. He had been forced to bed down in a tiny back room and lay wincing on a narrow bed as he tried to recover from his injuries. Quinn leaned over him and held up the silver deputy's badge.

'I can't afford a right hand man who appears weak in front of his men, Drake, so if you want this back you'll have to earn it.'

Drake struggled to sit up, groaning as he did so. 'I'll kill that bastard Barry, I swear it. Just give me the word, sir.'

'Not by yourself you won't. I don't want a repeat performance of what happened this afternoon.'

A look of low cunning passed across Drake's porcine features. 'I'll wait until tonight and take a couple of men with me. We'll just go in while he's sleeping and blast him to hell!'

Quinn nodded his approval. 'You can have your badge back when the job's done and there'll be a bonus too, say, a hundred dollars?'

Drake nodded his agreement and then gave a salute. 'You can rely on me, sir.'

'I hope so. I wouldn't want you to fail me again.'

There was an edge of menace in Quinn's tone and his subordinate shivered, despite the warmth of the day. Outside the door, Chiquita Sabatini stood listening in alarm before creeping upstairs to Sean's room where she knocked hesitantly before hearing the call to enter.

The marshal was pleasantly surprised by the sight of a beautiful young woman crossing the threshold of his room. Chiquita's jet-black hair, smooth olive skin and rounded figure often caused men's heads to turn and she was not surprised by his reaction. He frowned, however, when he saw the look of sadness in her large brown eyes and the expression of concern which furrowed her brow.

'Please forgive this intrusion but you are in grave danger.' Chiquita stood leaning against the door and he pulled up a chair, gesturing for her to sit down.

'Thank you, but there is no time for pleasantries. You must listen carefully to what I say. The man Drake will come with two others to kill you in this very room tonight.'

Chiquita clasped her hands in front of her and Sean covered them with his own in a gesture of reassurance. He guided her firmly over to the chair and gently pushed her down into it.

'Calm yourself, it won't be dark for several hours so we've plenty of time. Now, tell me who you are and how you came by this information.'

'I am Chiquita Sabatini and I heard Drake promise Quinn that he will do this.'

'I see, and why should this matter to you?'

She looked up at him imploringly. 'You are my only hope, Marshal. Only you can free me from this prison.'

Sean was bewildered. 'I don't understand. How are you imprisoned?'

Chiquita's face twisted into a grimace of hatred. 'That fiend Quinn forces me to be his woman. My father is a storekeeper here, a kind, gentle man who can hardly use a gun and does not know how to fight. Quinn said that unless I surrendered to his demands, he would give me to those animals he calls men, kill my father and burn his store to the ground.' Then she buried her face in a lace handkerchief and began to weep softly.

Sean knelt down in front her, his emotions a mixture of outrage at how she was treated and pity for her suffering. Chiquita looked up at him and their eyes met.

'Quinn makes me wear expensive jewels and I have some money saved, a few hundred dollars. I will give you everything I own if you promise to kill him.' She hesitated before continuing, 'You can have me too if you want, I'm not unattractive.'

Sean shook his head. 'You don't have to give me anything, Chiquita. If I demanded payment after hearing your story, I'd hardly be worthy of all those high hopes of yours, now would I?'

Then she smiled at him as she rose to her feet. 'No, I guess not. Bless you, you're a good man. Father Munro promised me you would come. He said he would send for you and now you are here.'

'I think it's Fr Munro who's the good man.'

'He comforts me when I talk to him about my troubles. If I ask for penance he tells me I already suffer enough.'

'I'm not a religious man but they sound like wise words to me.'

Chiquita nodded. 'I must go now before Quinn begins to wonder where I am. Be on your guard tonight.' Then she slipped away and was gone.

Drake chose Will Purcell and Hank Christianson to help him that night. Both men were light on their feet but strong and fast with a gun. He moved behind them stiffly as they crept up the staircase to Sean's room, each man with his pistol at the ready. Drake had earlier extracted the spare key from Turner by shoving the barrel of a gun into his mouth and threatening to pull the trigger. He passed it to Purcell, who slipped it carefully into the lock and turned it slowly so that the sound was barely discernible in the silence.

A sliver of moonlight illuminated the huddled shape under the bedclothes. The three men lined up inside the room and took aim. At a whispered command from Drake, they opened fire and let loose a hail of bullets. The huddled shape appeared to collapse in on itself and they stopped shooting when each of them had fired several times. Drake lit the lamp in the corner of the room and then pulled back the bedclothes. He stared dumbly for a moment at the pillows studded with bullet holes and the feathers which spilled out on to the bed.

Christianson and Purcell turned as Sean began shooting from behind, each crumpling to the floor with a bullet in his heart. Drake found his gun shot from his hand as he raised the barrel to fire and he immediately dropped to his knees.

'Don't shoot me, Marshal, please!' he whined. 'Quinn made me do it!'

'Yeah, I'm sure you took some persuading,' said Sean sarcastically. 'Give me one good reason why I shouldn't just kill you.'

'I . . . I . . . got information,' stammered Drake. 'There's a way outa here and nobody knows about it except me.'

Sean was intrigued. 'Go on. If what you have to say is of some use I'll let you live.'

'There's an old silver mine on the edge of town, ain't been worked for years cos all the silver's gone. Quinn sent me and another man, Petrie, to check it out when we first arrived. Petrie broke his neck when a shaft collapsed but it showed up a tunnel. I followed it and ended up outside, past the canyon. When I went back I didn't tell nobody about it.'

Sean frowned. 'Are you sure?'

Drake nodded eagerly. 'Yeah, I figured if things went sour I might need to get out in a hurry so I'd best keep it to myself. Quinn don't let his men leave town without permission.'

'A man on guard could see quite a way from the top of that canyon. How do you know you wouldn't be spotted?'

Drake shrugged. 'In the daytime you might be, but not at night. Now you can get away from here whenever you want. That ought to be worth my life.'

Sean agreed. 'OK but you leave through that tunnel tonight and if I ever see you again I'll kill you. Is that clear?'

Drake nodded ingratiatingly. 'Sure, Marshal. You won't see me no more, I promise.'

Sean holstered his gun as he turned away and the former sergeant seized an opportunity to grab his own weapon from the floor. Sensing the movement behind him, Sean spun around, took aim and squeezed the trigger before Drake had a chance to fire. The single shot caught him between the eyes and he fell back dead to the floor.

Sean looked down at the three dead men without pity. Quinn's hired killers had given him one simple choice: his life or theirs and the odds had hardly been weighed in his favour. The question now was how to take full advantage of what had happened and that might take some thought.

When morning came, the people of San Tomas were left in no doubt that Quinn's authority was being challenged. The three corpses were propped up in a standing position against the fountain. Each wore a placard with the inscription *I'll kill no more for Quinn*. Soon a small crowd gathered, pointing and whispering among themselves. They fell silent as Quinn and Luke Paterson pushed their way to the front. The ex-corporal stared at the bodies in disbelief and then turned to face the crowd, angrily drawing his gun.

'If anybody's got somethin' to say about this, come on out and say it! I ain't scared o' no marshal!'

There was a brief murmur but no one stepped forward and the crowd slowly melted away as Paterson continued to glare while making threatening gestures with his gun.

'Stay calm, Paterson. There's nothing to be gained by being hot headed,' Quinn warned him.

'I don't like this, sir. I don't like it one bit. This lawman's gonna get these folks all stirred up against us. Maybe we should think about clearin' out.'

Quinn looked up at him sharply. 'I'll decide when we leave. Is that clear?'

Paterson stiffened and gave a smart salute. 'Yes, sir!'

'Good. Now, is the next instalment ready yet?'

'The boys will have it all packed up tomorrow, sir.'

'Excellent; everything's going according to plan.' Quinn clapped his subordinate on the shoulder.

'Soon we'll have enough to buy up all the land and property we want back home. It'll be better than the old days, before the South lost and all those Yankee carpet-baggers moved in.'

Paterson grinned. 'I can hardly wait.' Then he added wistfully, 'I sure am sorry about my old pals though.'

'So am I. They were all good men, even Drake in his way. but don't you worry, Soldier. Marshal Sean Barry will get what's coming to him before we're finished here, I promise you. Now, get a burial detail together to put your fallen comrades in the ground.'

Sean watched from his window overlooking the fountain as Paterson marched off to do Quinn's bidding, then wondered about what he had just heard. There was clearly a long-term purpose to Quinn's stranglehold over the town and his extortion of money. Cash was being put together and taken away but where was it going? If he could find that out, Sean realized, a way might be found to defeat Quinn and his followers once and for all.

Then another figure walked across the square below, unmistakably that of Chiquita Sabatini. Quinn blocked her path as she reached the fountain and she stopped hesitantly in front of him. Sean heard him laugh mockingly.

'Off to talk to your friend the priest, my dear? Don't forget to tell him how cruel I've been!' Quinn called after her as she headed in the direction of the church. Sean waited until the sheriff had gone before leaving the hotel to follow her. Perhaps she knew something of Quinn's plans, some detail he might have let slip in an unguarded moment. If so, this would be the ideal opportunity to find out.

When Sean stepped inside the cool, candlelit interior of the church, Chiquita was sitting in the front pew. Father Munro was with her and the two were engaged in a whispered conversation. The priest looked up as Sean approached and gestured for him to join them.

'I can't say that I approve of your methods, Marshal. Parading dead bodies in the street is hardly civilized, is it?'

Sean shrugged. 'Those men tried to kill me and if it were not for Chiquita's warning I might be dead now. It was important to send Quinn a message and give some hope to the people of San Tomas.'

'Just be careful you don't become like your enemies while you do it.'

'Knock off the preaching, Father. I didn't come here for a sermon,' replied Sean irritably.

'Very well, what can I do for you?'

'It was Chiquita I actually came to see. I need to know what Quinn does with the plunder from this town. I heard him talking to Paterson about sending it away to buy land and property someplace.'

The girl frowned as she thought for a

moment. 'Silas tells me little of his plans but I know he's from Louisiana. Sometimes he forgets I am there and gives orders to his men in front of me. A few months ago he sent five of them away with a wagon. Now, where did they go?'

'This could be very important, Chiquita. Please try to remember,' Sean urged her.

There was a pause while she struggled to recall something. 'That's it!' she cried suddenly. 'I remember now. Silas said that everything was ready for the bank in Austin and I'm sure that was where they went.'

'There could be more than one bank in Austin,' remarked Munro.

'That doesn't matter just now. The point is that the next instalment is being transferred tomorrow and there's a chance to stop it before it even reaches Austin.'

'But you'd never get out of San Tomas alive!' declared Chiquita. 'Everyone leaving is seen by the men Silas has guarding the canyon.'

Then Sean told them about the secret tunnel under the abandoned mine which Drake had discovered.

'What are you going to do?' asked Chiquita anxiously.

'I'll leave by the tunnel tonight, ambush Quinn's men and bury the loot in the desert. Then I'll return under cover of darkness.'

'It will be five against one,' Munro warned him.

'I'll surprise them. Quinn is using his plunder to buy up land in Louisiana through the bank in Austin. This is the only way to stop him from bleeding San Tomas dry.'

'I don't like it. You'll be in great danger,' said Chiquita.

'Chiquita's right,' agreed Munro. 'However, there is someone I trust I could send with you. Would you like to meet him?'

'I'll shake hands with anyone willing to stand up to Quinn,' said Sean.

3

Pedro Hernandez owned a small cantina at the other end of town which was frequented by the Mexican inhabitants of San Tomas, the oldest of whom could remember a time when it belonged to Mexico. As Sean and his companions entered, Pedro was entertaining his customers with a love song which he sang while strumming a Spanish guitar. He was a short, wiry man in his thirties who sported a long moustache and a mass of dark curly hair.

Pedro flashed a smile and bowed in response to the applause which greeted him as he finished the song. He then stood up to greet the new arrivals.

'It is a pleasure to see you, Padre, and you, Chiquita. I am also honoured to meet the famous Marshal Sean Barry.'

'I didn't realize I was famous,' said

Sean as the two men shook hands.

'In San Tomas, *señor*, you are a hero!' declared Pedro and gestured towards a table covered by a red cloth. Then he called out in Spanish and a plump young woman appeared with two small children clinging to her skirts.

'Maria, bring tequila and tortillas for our esteemed guests!'

'There's really no need to go to all this trouble,' said Munro.

'It's not every day we have a hero in San Tomas who will stand up to Quinn and those scum he calls men.'

'I'm no hero,' Sean told him. 'I just don't like outlaws.'

'No one does, *señor*, but few people have the courage to stand up to them as you do.'

Maria brought food and drink to their table and the conversation stopped for a while as they tucked in. When they had finished eating, Munro stood up to go, declaring that he had duties to attend to but would leave the others to talk.

Pedro listened while Sean told him what he had learned about the money Quinn was collecting, the secret tunnel that led out of the canyon and his plan to make use of it.

'That is a bold strategy, very bold for just one man,' said Pedro as he poured them another glass of tequila.

'That's why Fr Munro was hoping you'd come with me.'

'The padre knows I fought with Juarez in Mexico, but that was several years ago,' sighed the Mexican. 'If I did not have Maria and the children to consider, I would go with you gladly but . . . ' His words trailed away as he winced with regret and drained his glass.

'I understand,' said Sean. 'I'm sorry. You have a young family and I shouldn't have asked you to put yourself at risk.'

At that moment, a shadow fell across the doorway as Paterson entered with two of Quinn's henchmen.

'Well, this looks friendly,' said the

corporal. Then his eyes narrowed when he saw Chiquita. 'I don't reckon Colonel Quinn will think much to you bein' here,' he said.

'I don't answer to you for where I go,' she replied disdainfully.

Paterson smiled as he stood over her. 'If you were mine, honey, I'd make you eat them words.'

'What do you want?' asked Pedro gruffly.

'It's time to pay up again, Hernandez. The price is thirty dollars.'

Pedro's eyes flashed angrily. 'Last month the price was twenty dollars and I couldn't afford that much!'

'Well, I figure you've been doin' pretty well lately so a little extra won't hurt. C'mon now, thirty dollars or the boys will smash the place up.'

Pedro rose abruptly to his feet and his chair crashed to the floor behind him. 'You damned thieving bastards!'

To Sean's surprise, Paterson merely laughed. 'He does this every time but then pays up like all the rest,' he told the men standing behind him.

'Maybe not today, Paterson. I think that Quinn's going to go a little short this month,' said Sean, as he stood up beside Pedro.

Paterson eyed Sean's pair of guns and licked his dry lips. 'I wouldn't be so sure,' he remarked, affecting an air of nonchalance he clearly did not feel.

'Does anyone want to try me?'

There was a long pause while Paterson and his men weighed up the situation. Then Sean spied a flicker of movement from the man on the corporal's right. The gang-member's gun was barely out of his holster when Sean's bullet hit him squarely between the eyes and he crumpled to the floor. The other one turned and fled while Pedro looked dumb-founded at the turn of events and hastily crossed himself as he looked down at the corpse.

Paterson stood his ground for a moment, a look of pure hatred in his eyes but fear overcame him and he did not go for his weapon.

'Are we just going to stand here like this all day?' asked Sean.

Paterson did not reply but turned to the doorway and called out 'Get your ass back in here, Stroud! The fun's over!'

His companion shuffled back in nervously and the corporal pointed wordlessly to the dead man on the floor. Stroud shouldered the corpse and Paterson followed him outside.

Chiquita shivered despite the warmth of the day. 'You haven't heard the last of this, either of you,' she warned them.

'No, Quinn will really start to get mad now which is all the more reason to fight,' agreed Pedro. Then he turned to Sean and asked, 'So, we leave tonight then?'

'I thought you weren't coming.'

'Today my eyes have been opened. I see what a man can do when he stops living on his knees.'

'What about your family?'

Pedro clapped him on the shoulder. 'They will understand. Besides, what kind of a husband and father can I be if I don't stand up for what's right? No, we will go together, *amigo*, and show Quinn that his days of ruling San Tomas are over.'

Knowing that Quinn might decide to send his men out in force to look for him following this latest escapade, Sean decided to hide out in the abandoned mine until nightfall. After a thorough search, he managed to locate the secret tunnel and followed its winding path until he reached an exit that led outside. Then he returned to the mine and settled down to wait. Pedro arrived just after sunset with their horses and provisions for the journey.

'Quinn has been turning the town upside down looking for you. He's convinced one of the towns-people has you hidden in an attic or cellar.'

'Let him look all he wants. By the time he figures out we've gone we'll be well on our way.'

Sean led the way, holding up a lantern and they led their horses slowly through the tunnel in the darkness. At last they reached the exit, mounted up and galloped away into the moonlit night and did not stop to rest until San Tomas was far behind them.

Meanwhile, Chiquita continued to resist Quinn's interrogation, protesting that she had no idea where Sean and Pedro were hiding.

'Come on, you were the last person to see Sean Barry, and Hernandez disappeared not long afterwards. Now, for the last time, where are they?'

'You're hurting me!' cried Chiquita, as Quinn tightened his grip on her arm. 'I've already told you, I know nothing!'

The sharp, stinging slap caught her by surprise and Chiquita's hand flew up to her cheek.

'I hope they kill you, you evil bastard!' she screamed.

Quinn's next blow sent her staggering across the room and she fell into a chair. He leaned over her and Chiquita shrank back from his gaze.

'Perhaps I should give you to my men

for the night. They may discover ways of persuading you to tell the truth. Of course, I won't have any use for you after that and no reason to keep your father alive either.'

Quinn's words were spoken softly, but the threat was all too real and she had no doubt that he would carry it out.

Chiquita fell to her knees, weeping and begging for forgiveness. 'Forgive me, Silas. I did not mean those harsh words and I would never dare to betray you!' She seized his hand and smothered it with her kisses. 'Please, if I knew anything I swear I'd tell you!'

Quinn abruptly pulled his hand away, a look of bored contempt on his face. 'Very well, I believe you. Now, you're getting hysterical over a little slap. Go wash your face and come back when you've calmed down.'

Chiquita quickly turned and fled from the room, but a smile of triumph played around her lips as she closed the door behind her. Her lover might continue to rant and rave for a while, then, once he realized he was not going to find the men he was looking for, he would get drunk. After that, the most unpleasant part of the evening would begin when she would have to endure his embraces. Then, finally, when he slept, she could put her own plan into action.

Out in the desert, dawn was breaking as Sean made coffee and fried beans for breakfast. Pedro sat up and tossed his blanket aside.

'That sure smells good,' he remarked as Sean passed him a plate of food and a steaming cup.

'Make the most of it. We've a hard ride ahead of us and then a tough fight when Quinn's men turn up.'

Their conversation was interrupted by the sound of galloping hoofs and both men reached for their guns. They quickly put them away as Chiquita came into view.

'What in hell are you doing here?' demanded Sean.

‘That’s no way to greet a friend,’ she said, as she jumped down from the saddle. ‘Besides, I’ve brought us some really good rifles.’

‘What do you mean, *us*? This is too dangerous for you. Go back before Quinn notices you’re missing.’

Chiquita was angry now. ‘Dangerous? You think you know all about danger, do you? How would you like your sister or your mother to have Quinn threaten them, beat them and force himself on them? Then, when they were lucky enough to escape, what would you think of the fool who told them to go back?’

She was standing close to Sean now and he finally noticed the bruises on each side of her face.

‘I’m sorry, Chiquita. I didn’t mean it like that. It’s just that there’s going to be a lot of shooting later and I don’t want you to get hurt.’

She shook her head defiantly. ‘If I’m going to die, I’d rather do it fighting Quinn than submitting to him.’

‘I think she’s right and it should be

her choice,' remarked Pedro.

'All right, let's have a look at these rifles of yours,' said Sean.

Chiquita proudly presented him with three Spencer repeating rifles and a box of cartridges. It was a weapon he had used during the Civil War while serving as a sergeant in the Union Army.

'Did I choose well?' she asked.

Sean nodded. 'You can get twenty rounds a minute out of one of these,' he said, stroking the barrel.

'I've never seen one before,' said Pedro, stepping closer.

'There's a lever here to take out the used shell and feed another cartridge into the tube. You cock the hammer manually,' explained Sean. Then he opened the weapon to show the seven-round tube magazine inside. 'You can fire rounds one after the other and then reload fast,' he continued.

'Where did you get these rifles?' asked Pedro.

'Quinn has a big supply of guns in his cellar so I just borrowed his keys while the pig was sleeping. He won't realize that I've taken them,' Chiquita replied.

'He'll notice you've gone when he wakes up and he won't like that,' said Sean, frowning. 'We'd better make for higher ground as soon as we've finished breakfast. My guess is that the men he sends to Austin with the money will be told to look for us as well. We'd better make sure we spot them first, or I don't reckon much to our chances.'

They ate and drank quickly before mounting up. Sean set a steady pace, anxious to maintain the gap between them and any pursuers. Then, as noon approached, Pedro spotted a low lying range and they headed straight for it. A narrow, winding path led them up between walls of rock that formed a canyon until they reached a plateau. A wide expanse of desert stretched out for miles below them.

'It's just the right place for an ambush, no?' said Pedro.

'Let's hope so,' replied Sean as they settled down to wait.

* * *

Back in San Tomas, Silas Quinn was as mad as hell when he awoke that morning to find Chiquita gone. Even the sight of £3,000 packed in a large cash box, silver plate and other valuables collected from the town's inhabitants, failed to lighten his mood.

'You'd better find Barry and that Mexican sidekick of his before you reach Austin,' he warned Paterson. 'When you get back I want to see proof that they're both dead.'

'What about the girl?'

'I want her alive. No woman runs out on me, and she'll learn that before I've finished with her.'

'I just can't understand how they escaped in the first place,' said the corporal.

'Those men you put up on that canyon must have been asleep,' snorted Quinn. 'I'm holding you personally responsible, Paterson, so don't fail me again.'

Paterson doubted that his men had been asleep but knew better than to argue with his boss. Quinn was quite capable of shooting him in cold blood if he got angry enough and he was almost as quick on the draw as Barry.

'I won't let you down, sir. I'll cut both their heads off and put 'em in a bag for you, how's that?'

'That would be most agreeable,' said Quinn, finally allowing himself a smile. 'Just make sure no one messes with Chiquita because I want her untouched. Is that clear?'

Paterson nodded and gave a smart salute as he prepared to drive away. Quinn had doubled the number of men accompanying the loot and would not accept any excuses for failure this time. Ten battle-hardened soldiers were being sent against two civilians and a girl. The corporal told himself that those odds ought to be more than good enough, despite the fear of the marshal that gnawed at his insides.

'Wait a minute, I have a little present

for you,' said Quinn suddenly. He called out, 'Bring the prisoner!' and the stooped, grey-bearded figure of Carlos Sabatini, Chiquita's father, was brought forward, shuffling towards the wagon in iron chains. Two men manhandled him on to the back and he sat down with a weary sigh of resignation.

'There, a little insurance for you, Paterson. They won't want to fire on the old man, will they? It should make your job even easier.'

The corporal clicked the reins over the horses' backs and the wagon was driven with its heavily armed escort out of San Tomas. Two men watched the departure with interest. Henry Cartwright had once been the respected mayor of San Tomas and Philip Bloom his deputy.

'How much did you have to pay this month, Philip?' asked Cartwright, as he lit his meerschaum pipe.

'Those damned rogues cost me a hundred dollars and it would have been more if Martha hadn't persuaded them to take that silver cutlery. We never did use it much anyway.' A short, rotund man, Bloom sweated easily in the heat and he removed his derby hat to wipe his bald dome with a large handkerchief. 'What about you, Henry?'

Cartwright removed his pipe and let out a sigh. Tall, thin and silver-haired, he had once cut an elegant figure around the town in his frock coat and stovepipe hat, but Quinn's depredations had greatly reduced his prosperity.

'Almost two hundred dollars in cash and a pocket watch. I've hardly anything valuable left for them to take.'

'It's got to stop, Henry, before we all become beggars.'

'Well, Quinn's just left himself ten men short and then there are the ones Barry killed, five altogether by my reckoning. Just now, our self-styled sheriff has fifteen fewer men than he had the day he came here.'

'That's quite a difference,' remarked Bloom. 'Do you think it would work now, the plan we discussed?'

Cartwright nodded as he drew on his pipe. 'This is probably the best chance we have. Go talk to the others, but be discreet. We'll meet this evening in the usual place.'

The two men parted and went their separate ways. A small group of concerned citizens had met sporadically in secret ever since Quinn came to San Tomas. A plan for an armed rebellion against his rule had slowly taken shape, but the time had never seemed right to attempt it. Those willing to risk their lives were always outnumbered by the forces at Quinn's disposal but now the odds had improved. Finally, it seemed, the people of the town were about to stand up for themselves.

* * *

Sean waited anxiously with his companions on the plateau, squinting through his old army telescope into the harsh glare of sunlight to see what was coming. Finally, he spotted a cloud of dust approaching in the desert below and made out the figure of Paterson driving the wagon. He counted the number of men.

'Are they coming?' asked Pedro urgently.

'Yeah, it's them all right but there's ten altogether, more than we expected. Get ready to fire.' Then he saw the prisoner on the back of the wagon. 'That's strange, there's an old guy chained up, a Mexican with a beard.'

'Let me see!' cried Chiquita and he passed the telescope to her. 'It's my father! We'd better not shoot!'

'That's what they want you to think, Chiquita. Then what will happen to your father afterwards? You know Quinn will not just let him go,' Pedro told her.

'He's right,' added Sean. 'Your father's best chance is for us to try to free him. Now, they're coming, so let's just be extra careful when we aim.'

Chiquita nodded wordlessly and they all prepared to fire. Sean's first shot hit the man sitting beside Paterson in the chest and he tumbled from the wagon with a groan. Another man guarding Carlos Sabatini tried to haul the hapless prisoner to his feet to use him as a shield, but Chiquita went for a head shot and he fell back with a cry. Sean then raked the cluster of outriders behind the wagon with a rapid series of shots and several tumbled from their horses.

Pedro noticed that Paterson was now lashing the horses furiously to escape, abandoning the rest of his men in the process. One of them, whose mount had been shot from under him, was desperately running to catch up and jump on the back. Pedro blasted him and then shot away the axle on the wagon so that it was forced to a grinding halt. Paterson leaped nimbly to the ground, however, narrowly evading the bullet meant for him.

By this time, Paterson's remaining men had abandoned their horses and made for the shelter of some rocks lower down where they began to spread out and return fire. Bullets ricocheted around Sean as he ducked down to avoid being hit.

'They're trying to get round behind us,' warned Chiquita as she narrowly missed a figure dodging between some rocks below her to the left.

'I've got an idea,' said Sean, spotting a large boulder to his right. 'Just keep down and squeeze behind this big rock next to me.'

The others did as he asked and then, at his command, they heaved with all their might. The boulder rolled down the cliff below, setting off a massive rock fall and a panic among their attackers who were forced to flee for their lives. Two were crushed by falling rocks as they scrambled in a mêlée to escape. Two more were cut down by the hail of gunfire Sean unleashed after them. He sensed a movement to his left and blasted a hole in the chest of the last man standing who had somehow reached the path leading up to the plateau.

'Well, it seems like we've won,' said Sean and the others followed as he set off down towards the wrecked wagon below.

'That's far enough!' called Paterson, as he emerged from behind the shelter of the broken wagon, holding a gun to Carlos Sabatini's head as Chiquita gasped with horror.

4

'Let him go and we won't shoot you,' said Sean.

'Not so fast, Marshal. I want a horse and a saddlebag filled with money from that cashbox. Then I'll release the old man.'

'That money doesn't belong to you,' Sean told him, 'but you can go free if you release Señor Sabatini.'

'No deal. Give me what I want, or I'll blow his head off!'

'He's bluffing,' said Pedro. 'If Paterson does that he knows we'll kill him.'

'No, don't take chances with my father's life!' said Chiquita. 'Give him what he wants, please!'

'All right,' said Sean reluctantly, and he turned to shoot the lock off the cashbox. At that moment, a shot rang out and the pistol fell from Paterson's numbed fingers as he sank to the ground, his features frozen in an expression of surprise.

'Drop those rifles! You're surrounded,' a voice called out from a rocky outcrop behind the broken wagon.

Then Sean looked up and saw a line of armed men standing at the very top of the canyon, above the plateau. More emerged from a cave behind them at the foot of the range and he saw that they were all Mexicans. Then, finally, the man who had called out approached them, holding a pistol in each hand as Sean and his companions dropped their weapons.

'Allow me to introduce myself, *señors*. I am Luis Chavez and these are my men.' He then looked at Chiquita approvingly and gave a short bow. 'It is a particular pleasure to meet you, *señorita*.' She ignored him however, and ran to embrace her father.

As Chavez came closer, Sean noticed his unusual appearance. He wore a red silk shirt beneath the bandoleer across his chest and boots of the finest leather.

His smooth round face was cleanly shaven and, when he grinned, their captor displayed several gold teeth.

'What do you want?' Sean asked him.

'Why that is very simple. I merely wish to take what you were about to steal yourselves. You should be grateful to me for relieving you of the burden of committing a very grave sin!' Then he laughed uproariously at his own joke.

'Is this what you have become now, Luis, a bandit?' It was Pedro who spoke and Chavez appeared to recognize him, his eyes widening in surprise. The two men exchanged a brief conversation in Spanish while Sean looked on in puzzlement.

'We fought together against the Emperor Maximilian and his French allies,' explained Pedro.

'Unfortunately the revolution did not deliver all it promised,' added Chavez in a tone of regret.

'He means that being on the right side did not make him rich,' said Pedro, bitterly.

'When I spoke to him just now, Pedro told me that you were taking this money back from people who had stolen it. Is that true?' asked Chavez.

'Yes, we're not bandits like you.'

The Mexican adopted an expression of mock sympathy. 'What can I say? I am sorry you are not also thieves for then you would have no cause to complain,' and his men all joined in the laughter.

Pedro stepped forward towards his old comrade. 'I saved your life once, Chavez, when we fought together. Is this how you repay me?'

'You can join us and have a share if you want,' replied the bandit with a shrug.

Pedro spat contemptuously on the ground. 'What about the people to whom this treasure really belongs? They are ruled over by a tyrant, worse than Maximilian whom we fought against. Half of them are our own people, not only gringos.'

'What do you want me to do, cry

about it?' demanded Chavez angrily. 'When the revolution was over I got a piece of land, sure, but you try scratching a living from it. All those generals who sided with Juarez got estates and government jobs.'

At that moment, Carlos Sabatini stepped away from his daughter, his chains clinking. 'I know what I would like you to do, *señor*. I want you to fight in a good cause as you did in the past. When you were a soldier you were paid to fight, no?'

Chavez nodded as he eyed the old man suspiciously. 'What about it?'

'Well, maybe you could take some of this money as payment to free San Tomas from the men who stole it, the same men who put me in these chains. You must have watched my daughter and her friends fight, yet you did nothing. Why not do something to earn your bread instead of just taking it from the mouths of others?'

Chavez was silent for a moment while he considered this. 'There is something in what you say, old man.'

'You have about twenty men and Quinn can't have many more than that left. I'd say the odds are good,' Sean told him. 'It would probably mean just a day's work.'

Chavez frowned thoughtfully. 'This Quinn, is it Silas Quinn you are talking about?'

'Yes, do you know him?'

'I've heard of this Southern gringo before, how he massacred peasants during the revolution. If there's enough cash in that box to give us a hundred dollars each you have a deal, I promise you.'

'There should be. Quinn's been stealing money and valuables from the people of San Tomas for months, stashing it all away in a bank in Austin while buying up land in Louisiana.'

Chavez turned and shot the lock off the cashbox and then opened it. He gestured to two of his men who stepped forward to count the bundles of cash.

The bandit leader put his pistols

away once he learned how much there was. 'Two thousand dollars will cover what we agreed. The rest can be given back to the people of San Tomas. Does that sound fair to you?'

'We'll bury the money and the other stuff out here for now. You'll get paid when the job's done,' Sean told him.

'You are in no position to make demands, *señor*. We will take what is owed to us in advance,' said Chavez.

'Let him have it his way,' advised Pedro. 'He could have shot us and just taken everything if he had really wanted to.'

'That's right. I wouldn't forget that if I were you,' added Chavez, with a sly smile. He then proceeded to distribute the money among his followers, also helping himself to the Spencer rifles, while Sean, Pedro and Chiquita packed the rest of the money and the various items of silverware in their saddlebags. Carlos had his chains removed and he was provided with a horse before they all set off back to San Tomas.

'Will Chavez keep his word?' Sean asked Pedro, as the two men rode along together.

'I don't see any reason why not, but Luis is an opportunist and he never reveals what he is thinking. He can do you a good turn if it suits him, but he is just as likely to stab you in the back.'

Sean sighed. 'Why do I feel as if I've just made a pact with the devil?' he asked.

Back in San Tomas, a small group of leading citizens were meeting in the church. They were all holding prayer books as if attending a service, just in case one of Quinn's men should enter, but it was Henry Cartwright who addressed them.

'My friends, I've called you here because I think we now have a real chance to take back control of our town. As you know, Sean Barry killed five of Quinn's men while he was here and ten others have left in pursuit of him and our fellow citizens, Pedro Hernandez and Chiquita Sabatini.

Quinn now has barely twenty men to support him and I believe we should strike tonight while they're asleep.'

'There'll be guards on duty,' warned George Donaldson, a short, wiry individual who owned the livery stables.

'We have the means to overpower them because their coffee will have been drugged,' replied Cartwright.

'What about those other ten men? They'll be coming back, won't they?' asked Alberto Garcia nervously. He was thinking of his precious hardware store and the possibility that it could be burned down.

'Perhaps not,' said Munro before Cartwright had a chance to reply. 'Marshal Barry and Señor Hernandez left town secretly in the hope that they could ambush Quinn's men and get back what they stole. There is, apparently, a secret tunnel running under the mine which allowed them to make their escape at night.'

'There,' said Cartwright. 'If they've succeeded, we have less to worry about than we thought. If not, then we must be ready to surprise Quinn's remaining men upon their return.'

'As a priest, I do not normally condone violence but Quinn and his men are evil,' Munro told them. 'Evil must be fought in order to safeguard what is good and those who are attacked have a right to defend themselves. However, if possible you should try to arrest these men and lock them up. Then they can be put on trial for their crimes.'

Cartwright nodded his approval. 'I agree, Father. We're not a mob bent on revenge. Remember, if we agree to do this, we must shoot only when necessary and not in cold blood.'

'I propose we take a vote now,' suggested Philip Bloom. 'Personally, I'm in favour of going ahead.'

Cartwright asked for a show of hands and it was clear that only two people favoured continuing to wait. 'All right,' he declared briskly, 'you all know the plan and we start at midnight.'

There was a knock at Quinn's door

just after sundown and one of his men answered it. As Bloom stood on the threshold he was searched for weapons and then allowed to enter.

'Was that really necessary?' asked the former deputy mayor, as the door was closed behind him.

'I can't be too careful. Besides, a man who double crosses once can always do it again.'

Bloom shrugged. 'I know where my interests lie and I've no intention of getting my ass shot off.'

'At least not without getting paid for it, anyway,' replied Quinn, as he held up a wad of cash. 'Now, what have you got to tell me?'

'Cartwright and the others have decided to go ahead with their plan at midnight.' He paused, eyeing the money greedily.

'Go on,' Quinn urged him. 'Give me the full details.'

'It's the plan I told you about before. Ten armed men will enter the hotel and arrest you and the others at gunpoint.

The woman who brings the guards their coffee is in on it. Their drinks will have been drugged.'

'We'll deal with that bitch later. What happens then?'

'You're all to be locked up in the jail. There'll be a trial and then a lot of hangings.'

Quinn tossed Bloom the wad of cash and he counted it quickly. 'There's something else if you're interested. I thought it might be worth a little bonus.'

The traitor suddenly found himself staring down the barrel of a gun. 'I've just given you three hundred dollars, you greedy rat. If you have anything more to say I strongly suggest you start saying it. Otherwise I might add to your fee in lead.'

Bloom paled visibly. 'There's a way out of here through a tunnel in the old mine. You can get out beyond the canyon. That's how Barry and his friends escaped.'

'How did you find that out?'

demanded Quinn.

'The priest told us about it tonight. I don't know where he got the information from.'

'Munro's more dangerous than I thought. Is that all?'

'There's just one other thing: Munro said that Barry and Hernandez were planning to ambush Paterson's men.'

'Two against ten, not very good odds I'd say,' murmured Quinn.

'The Sabatini woman might have caught up with them. I've heard she's a good shot.'

Bloom was silent for a moment and Quinn stared at his informant. 'Are you calculating the odds, Bloom, and figuring whether to change sides again?'

'Why should I? Even if the worst happens and Barry kills all your men before coming back to start trouble, you'll have fixed all the people who might help him.'

'That's right and don't you forget it. Now go on, get out of here.'

As Bloom scurried from the room,

Quinn sat back and considered what sort of reception he should prepare for his assailants. Then he told the guard who had admitted Bloom to spread the word discreetly among the men. There was to be no liquor tonight, but those on duty were to drink their drugged coffee and show no sign that they knew anything of what was about to happen. Cartwright and his friends were in for a big surprise, especially the priest. It was about time he was dealt with once and for all.

Cartwright assembled his followers behind the stables at midnight, as arranged. 'If anyone wants to pull out, now's the time to do it,' he told them. He paused for a moment but his words were met with silence and expressions of grim determination. Even the usually timid Garcia looked fierce, his knuckles white as he gripped a pistol in his hand.

'Come on, let's get going,' urged Bloom, and they set off cautiously down the main street towards the hotel.

The two men sitting outside were

slumped over their rifles, snoring under the starlight. Bloom remained outside, supposedly to guard them in case they woke up and also to watch for anyone coming down the street.

The others entered and began to cross the saloon, dimly lit by a couple of lamps turned down low and shafts of moonlight that filtered through the windows. The shooting started before they reached the stairs. Quinn's men stood up from behind the bar and the pillars where they had been hiding and kept firing until not one of their enemies remained standing. Bullets ricocheted around the room, shattered glasses and embedded themselves in the walls but also thudded into the twisting bodies of Cartwright and his men. The air was thick with smoke while the cries of the dying were almost as loud as the sound of gunfire. When it stopped there was an eerie silence, broken only by the occasional muffled groan.

The lamps were turned up and Quinn stepped among the fallen bodies, turning them over with his foot. Most were dead but Cartwright had been hit in the leg and was now struggling into an upright position while Garcia was slumped against the wall, clutching a wounded arm.

'We'll keep these two alive,' said Quinn. 'I've got plans for them.'

Cartwright's hand crept towards a pistol lying near him but Quinn brought his boot down heavily on the man's fingers and he gasped in pain.

'You don't learn, do you?'

'I'll never stop fighting you, Quinn, as long as there's breath in my body.'

'Well, you won't have that for much longer.' The colonel turned to his men. 'See to their wounds and put them in the jail. It would be a shame if they died before we got around to hanging them, wouldn't it?'

Bloom stood watching beside Quinn as the injured men were hauled outside, stepping back when Cartwright turned to stare at him.

'How could you do this to us, to

people you've known for years?' asked the former mayor incredulously.

Bloom shrugged. 'A man's got to look out for his own interests. Besides, you never stood a chance.'

'The people of San Tomas aren't stupid. They'll get to know what you did and when they do you'd better keep looking over your shoulder,' Cartwright told him.

'I shall pray that I live long enough to see you die with a knife in your back,' added Garcia as he spat upon the ground in contempt.

'Well it won't be you putting it there!' called Bloom as the two men were hustled away.

'Somebody will,' Quinn added quietly.

The former deputy mayor paled visibly. 'What do you mean?'

'Word gets around. It might not be safe for you here much longer.'

'You could protect me though. I've been useful, haven't I?'

Quinn looked at the traitor's round, sweating face with distaste. 'My men have got better things to do than play nursemaid, but you could earn yourself some more money before you have to clear out.'

Bloom licked his dry lips nervously. 'How much are we talking about?'

'This is a little dangerous so I think it's worth a thousand dollars. Added to the rest of the money I've paid you over the past year, it ought to be enough to provide a comfortable start in a new place.'

'What do I have to do to earn it?'

Bloom then listened anxiously as Quinn outlined his plan. Neither man was aware that Munro stood flattened against the wall of the hotel. Once he had heard what he needed to know, he crept away silently. Quinn would be coming for him soon enough and he needed to be ready.

* * *

The heat of the day gave way to a cool breeze as Sean and his companions halted in the amber glow of dusk. Chavez busied himself with orders to his men about making camp and who was to take the first watch. He carried himself with a certain swagger and approached Chiquita, offering to help her down from her horse.

'I can manage,' she told him stiffly.

'There is a comfortable spot over there where we might share a blanket, if the *señorita* will permit,' he said, apparently undaunted by her coldness towards him.

'I have my own blankets.'

'Perhaps your heart will soften towards me when I kill this Quinn for you, eh? Then you can be my woman and I will treat you better than he has done, that I promise you!'

'One bandit is no better than another as far as I'm concerned,' Chiquita told him haughtily as she turned away from him.

Suddenly her wrist was seized and Chavez spun her around to face him again. 'I can wait but you will be my woman. That much is certain.'

'I don't think the lady welcomes your attentions, Chavez,' Sean warned him as he approached the bandit leader.

Chavez released Chiquita and she moved away from him quickly but he stood his ground as Sean moved closer.

'You're being paid to do a job and that doesn't include bothering her. Do I make myself clear?'

'Perfectly, *señor*, but I don't take orders from gringos. So, do you want to fight me for her?'

Sean shrugged. 'She can make up her own mind about who she wants, if anybody. Besides, we need you to free San Tomas and it won't help if we start fighting among ourselves.'

Chavez nodded. 'You are wise, *señor*, but if you continue to interfere, the time will come when I shall have to kill you and that would be a pity.'

'You will have to kill me too before you lay another hand on my daughter.' Both men turned as Carlos stepped out of the shadows to join them. 'I saw what happened and I must warn you that I will not permit it.'

Chavez threw back his head and his whole body shook with laughter. 'So, the old man will not permit it, eh? That's a good one!'

'I admit that I am not much of a fighter, but I have allowed too much to befall Chiquita as it is. No, I cannot fight, but I can kill. I could stab you in your sleep, or creep up behind you and cave in your skull with a rock. A man protecting the most precious thing he has, his own flesh and blood, cares little for his own life so beware, *señor*.'

The old man spoke quietly and with dignity. There was no mistaking the seriousness of his intent and, as Carlos turned away, the bandit leader's laughter turned into silence.

That same night, Quinn entered the church, accompanied by two of his men. The candles on the altar were lit and a cassocked figure knelt in prayer before it. The colonel smiled to himself. He would enjoy stringing up Munro with his friends after all the trouble he had caused.

'Come on, Father. It will soon be time to meet your Maker.'

There was no response and Quinn reached out to seize the priest's shoulder. The figure then slid sideways, turning over as it hit the floor and the three men found themselves staring at the face of a straw dummy, the features painted in an expression of surprise.

'Find him, damn it! I don't care if you have to tear this whole town apart, just find him!'

As the two men ran to do their boss's bidding, Munro was already riding far into the desert, his horse snorting cold air under the pale moonlight. He had to find Sean Barry and the others to warn them about the reception Quinn was preparing. Spurring his horse to go a little faster, he prayed that he would not be too late.

5

Philip Bloom was more than an hour's ride ahead of Munro. Despite his rotund appearance, he had been an expert horseman in his youth as well as a highly skilled tracker and cattle rustler. These abilities had enabled him to generate wealth, pose as a respectable citizen and carve out a position of importance in San Tomas. The arrival of Quinn had necessitated a return to his criminal ways, for it was only by turning informer that he had managed to avoid the losses incurred by Cartwright and the other fools who followed the former mayor's lead. This last job would put an end to all that and soon he could make a new start somewhere else. Barry was a resourceful man, not unlike himself, and Bloom had little doubt that he and his friends had successfully ambushed that bonehead

Paterson. He just hoped that he could persuade the marshal to walk into Quinn's trap. Then it would all be over and he could head off to a more peaceful life over the border.

Sean awoke at first light and sat up. He was surrounded by sleeping figures and the sound of snoring emerged from the shapes huddled under blankets. Chavez and his men had been drinking and playing cards late into the night and he guessed they would not wake for a while yet. The smell of hot coffee and beans assailed his nostrils and he turned to see that Chiquita was already up. She smiled when she saw him and handed him a steaming cup.

'I couldn't sleep, knowing that pig Chavez wasn't far away.'

'Don't worry about him. He's been warned off,' Sean told her as he sipped the hot liquid gratefully.

'That sure smells good.' The words were spoken by a short, fat man leading a magnificent horse behind him.

Sean's hand hovered near his holster

and the stranger hesitated when he saw the gesture.

'Take it easy, Marshal. I'm Philip Bloom, used to be deputy mayor of San Tomas before Quinn showed up.'

'It's all right, Sean, I recognize him,' added Chiquita.

Sean extended his hand in greeting. 'I'm sorry, Mr Bloom. I find it pays a man to be cautious.'

'Think nothing of it,' replied Bloom as the two men shook hands. Then he looked around nervously at Sean's sleeping companions. 'Who are they?'

'A bunch of bandits led by a man called Chavez. They're being paid to help rid San Tomas of Quinn and his followers.'

'I see,' said Bloom cautiously. 'Did they help you out with Paterson's men?'

'No, they just watched while Pedro, Chiquita and me shot it out with them. Then they tried to take the money and other stuff Quinn stole, but we managed to make a deal with them.'

Bloom smiled as Chiquita handed

him a tin cup full of coffee. 'Well, you don't need to worry about that now. The folks in San Tomas staged a fight back, killed a number of Quinn's men and put the rest in jail. That's what I rode out here to tell you.'

Pedro had also awoken and was helping himself to coffee and a plate of beans. 'Does that mean we can get rid of Chavez and his cutthroats?'

'It might not be a bad idea. After all, you don't need them now and they're not the sort of people we want in town, having just got rid of one bunch of thieves.'

'It's a pity we've already paid them,' said Sean.

Bloom shrugged. 'It's not important. The main thing is, San Tomas is free and that's largely down to you, Marshal. We all saw how you stood up to Quinn and your example inspired the rest of us. I'm here to tell you that we're holding a fiesta and you're going to be the guest of honour. You and your friends are to come back with me and ride in triumph through the centre of the town. Now, how does that sound?'

'That sounds most agreeable, *señor*.' The words came from Chavez who had woken from his slumbers and had been listening to their conversation. 'It would only be polite to invite us, no?'

'You've got your money, Chavez. Now all you have to do to earn it is to leave us alone,' Sean told him.

The bandit leader shook his head. 'No, you paid us to do a job and we will not leave without seeing for ourselves if it needs to be done.' Then his eyes narrowed as he stared hard at Bloom. 'Besides, I do not trust this gringo. I have seen him someplace before and I never forget a face.'

'Have it your way,' Sean told him. 'You'll only be wasting your time.'

'We shall see, *señor*, we shall see,' replied Chavez slowly, still without taking his eyes off Bloom. Then he turned and began kicking his men awake, ignoring their groans and curses. 'Wake up, you dogs! We have a fiesta to go to!'

* * *

Meanwhile, Munro was sitting some miles away, crouched over the remains of a camp-fire. He picked up a discarded cigar stub and sniffed it, guessing that Bloom had rested here for a few hours before dawn. He made himself some coffee and settled down to wait. It was not long before his acute hearing picked up the sound of hoofs approaching in the distance and his whole body tensed as he stood up.

Munro was not wearing clerical garb and Bloom did not recognize him as he approached. The former deputy mayor was riding in front, leading the way back to San Tomas and drew to a halt as the priest stood in front of his horse, barring his way.

'What do you want?'

Munro stepped closer and Bloom swallowed hard before trying to hide his anxiety with bluster.

'I'm surprised to see you out here,

Father. Shouldn't you be looking after your parish?'

'That's just what I am doing, Bloom, protecting it from the likes of you.'

'I . . . I don't know what you mean, you must have gone crazy,' stammered Bloom. 'Look at him, out here dressed like a gunslinger. Don't pay any attention to what he says,' he told the others.

Bloom's hand strayed towards his gunbelt, but he stopped suddenly when Sean's pistol was poked into his ribs.

'I'd be very interested in hearing what Fr Munro has to say,' said the marshal.

'I think we all would,' added Pedro.

'Bloom's leading you into a trap. Quinn's men are to shoot you down as you ride into the centre of town. The uprising he told you about failed, thanks to his betrayal. Only two of the rebels, Henry Cartwright and Alberto Garcia, survived and Quinn plans to hang them as a warning to the townspeople.'

'That's nonsense . . . he's crazy, I tell you — '

'Be quiet!' Sean told Bloom, pressing the gun more firmly into the traitor's plump flesh.

'Now I remember this gringo!' cried Chavez. 'He sold horses to both sides during the war in Mexico and later, guns, too.'

'So what if I did? That doesn't prove anything!' protested Bloom.

'It proves you can't be trusted,' said Pedro.

'Let's kill him!' demanded Chavez.

'No, I think he could be of some use,' declared Sean. 'Quinn expects to see him lead us into town so maybe we should let him do just that but you, Chavez, and your men here will be the ones to provide the surprise.'

The bandit leader grinned, showing his gold teeth. 'I like your way of thinking, *señor*. I like it very much. When this is over, maybe you'll join me, eh?'

'I prefer to stay on the right side of the law.'

Chavez chuckled and turned his attention to the priest. 'You don't look much like a padre in that fancy suit.'

Munro swung himself into the saddle of his horse. 'A cassock's not much use on an errand like this,' he said.

'Holy Mother, you're wearing a gun too!' Chavez adopted a mock expression of disapproval and crossed himself ostentatiously.

'It belonged to my late brother,' explained Munro. 'I hope I won't have to fire it.'

Bloom was relieved of his gun and his hands were bound to his horse's saddle as they set off once more on their journey to San Tomas. He sat scowling on his mount but made no further attempts to claim innocence, realizing that it was hopeless.

'If I didn't know better, I'd swear I was riding with George Munro and not his saintly brother,' Sean told the priest.

'I make no claim to sainthood, Marshal.'

'The people of San Tomas might, on

your behalf, I mean.'

Munro shrugged. 'I'm just a man doing his best, Marshal, not unlike you.'

'What about that gun you're wearing? Are you really prepared to use it?'

Munro sighed. 'I guess I won't know that until the time comes, but if it's a choice between the lesser of two evils, then I probably will.'

Sean shook his head in puzzlement. 'I can't imagine there are many priests like you, Father. You're a hard man to fathom.'

Munro smiled enigmatically. 'Perhaps that's because you don't know many priests.'

Shortly afterwards they came to a fork in the road and Sean consulted his map. 'If we take the right fork we come to a small village on the border. I'm hoping we can buy a wagon there.'

'Is that for Chavez and his men to hide in?' Chiquita asked.

Sean nodded. 'If we can get one it will be worth the detour.'

'Your Trojan horse trick won't work, Barry,' Bloom warned him. 'Give it up, man. Let me go into San Tomas and talk to Quinn. He'll be willing to do a deal when he knows you've got reinforcements.'

'Forget it. I'm not stupid enough to let you warn him so he can prepare another trap. No, you'd better hope this works because you'll be driving that wagon with a gun pointed at your back. Just remember, if it goes wrong, you'll be the first to get a bullet.'

Bloom fell back into a morose silence as they took the right fork and headed towards the village. It had grown up around the ruins of an old monastery and amounted to little more than a row of houses along a dusty street, a saloon and a blacksmith's shop. The blacksmith was a burly individual in a leather apron who stood hammering away at his forge. He looked up as Sean approached.

'What can I do for you, mister?'

'I was hoping someone here might have a wagon for sale.'

'Usually the answer would be no. This place ain't worth a spit, but today you're in luck. I had me a customer who couldn't pay enough in cash so left me a wagon, but I got no use for it.'

Sean followed him around to the back of the shop. The vehicle looked old but sturdy enough to take the weight of twenty men. The cover was worn and patched in places but would certainly hide those travelling in the back.

'How much do you want for it?'

The blacksmith shrugged. 'The man who left it owed me ten dollars.'

Sean paid him and they set about preparing the vehicle for departure, hitching up six horses to the front while Chavez looked longingly towards the saloon.

'This calls for a little celebration, I think.'

'You can celebrate when the job's done,' Sean told him.

'I don't like to be told what to do, especially not by some gringo lawman.' Chavez had adopted a defiant, surly tone and was clearly aware of his men watching to see who would win the confrontation. The Mexican's hand twitched slightly, but before he could even decide to draw, he found himself staring down the barrel of Sean's gun.

'If you kill me, my men will avenge the death. Who will fight for San Tomas then?'

Suddenly Munro was standing between the two of them. 'If Señor Chavez agreed that he and his men could have just one drink, would that be acceptable?'

Sean considered the compromise for a moment. Chavez could not afford to back down in front of his men and Munro's suggestion allowed him to save face. 'All right, let's all have just one drink.' He lowered the pistol as the bandit leader grunted his assent and walked towards the saloon. Pedro and Chiquita both stayed with the wagon.

As they approached the batwings, they noticed a man in a dusty soldier's uniform lounging outside. He was unshaven and held a bottle of whisky in one hand from which he took a generous swig.

'How about takin' that drink with me and my pals inside?' he enquired.

'Sure,' agreed Chavez. 'A man should always be sociable when he drinks.'

As they stepped over the threshold, Sean saw about a dozen other uniformed men sitting around tables. They all appeared dusty, dishevelled and unshaven with no man above the rank of corporal.

'You're a long way from any fort. Where's your commanding officer?'

'Oh we had a little difference of opinion with Lieutenant Morse, didn't we, Krebs?' remarked one of the men with a bitter laugh.

The soldier who had been standing by the doorway joined in the laughter. 'Yeah, that's right. You see our heroic young officer was rather too keen on fightin' Apaches so some of us decided on a little private enterprise.'

'You're deserters in other words,' said Munro.

Krebs scratched his bristled chin and took a swig from the bottle he carried. 'I guess so, but with a purpose you boys might be interested in.'

Chavez and his followers now clustered eagerly around the bar. 'If there is money to be made, *señor, my* men will certainly be interested.'

Krebs nodded. 'That's good to hear, amigo. Our esteemed lieutenant and former comrades were guardin' a payroll when we were all attacked by them Apaches I mentioned. Things weren't lookin' too good so we skedaddled here to a position we could defend. I reckon Morse and the others will have been finished off by now so the Apaches will follow our tracks and head here after us.'

'What about the money?'

'That's the hard part,' said Krebs. 'We'll have to fight the Apaches for what's in that big iron cashbox, at least ten thousand dollars, I'd say.'

'Let me get this straight: you ran away from the Apaches and left your comrades to die but now you want us to help you fight them in return for stolen money,' said Sean in disgust.

Krebs appeared unmoved. 'I wouldn't call it runnin' away exactly, more of a tactical retreat. You see there were more than thirty of them Apaches and we left Morse with ten men. They'll kill a few before they get wiped out so our combined forces should outnumber 'em now.'

Chavez nodded thoughtfully. 'There is much in what you say and we have buildings to provide cover here.'

Sean shook his head. 'This is crazy, Chavez. We should get out of here while we have the chance.'

'We might think you were bein' a mite unfriendly if you did that, wouldn't we, Krebs?' The man who had spoken had a squat, burly frame and his tunic was half undone. The scarred face beneath the dome of his bald head suggested he was a veteran of many battles. 'Those Apaches will be headin' this way whether you like it or not. We can't hope to outrun 'em so we gotta stand and fight. Once they've been here, they'll follow any tracks they find and maybe catch up with you too.'

'That's right, Clancy,' agreed Krebs, turning to face Sean. 'So, it might not be wise to get unfriendly now, would it?'

Before Sean could answer he heard a shot followed by a scream from outside. He turned and looked through the grimy window of the saloon to see Chiquita trying to fight off the advances of a bearded soldier. The blacksmith lay dead on the ground, presumably having been shot for trying to intervene, while another grinning deserter stood with a rifle pointed at the helpless Pedro. Carlos sat slumped on the ground, bleeding from a head wound.

'Call off your men, Krebs. We'll all stay to help,' urged Sean with a sigh of resignation.

'Hey, let the girl go, Hunter!' shouted Krebs and the soldier reluctantly released Chiquita. Sean stepped out of the saloon and she ran into his arms, Pedro stepped away from the man with a rifle who had reluctantly lowered his weapon and looked on in puzzlement as Sean comforted Chiquita.

'What's going on in this place?'

Munro stepped out to join them and explained what had happened inside the saloon. 'I think the townspeople hid indoors when the soldiers arrived and probably know nothing about what's going to happen. At least this gives us a chance to help protect them from the Apaches,' he added.

'It looks like you'll get a chance to find out whether you can use that gun or not, Padre,' said Pedro ruefully.

'Would you do me a favour? No priestly titles until we get back to San Tomas.'

'Sure,' said Pedro, as he watched Munro walk away. There was something different in his stride and in the confident way he began to check his pistol that left the Mexican wondering whether there was a side to the priest he knew nothing about. Dismissing the thought from his mind, he turned to help the injured Carlos to his feet.

Krebs estimated that the Apaches would probably arrive within a couple of hours. 'That depends on how long our little tin soldier, Morse, managed to hold 'em off,' he added, grinning. He and Chavez then spread their men out so that they took cover inside the various buildings. The village's inhabitants were informed of what was happening and some opted to stay and fight while others fled, or hid in cellars.

Sean, Munro, Pedro, Chiquita and a bandaged Carlos all took cover among the ruins of the monastery. They took Bloom with them and it was reluctantly agreed that he should be untied and given a gun.

'Just remember, if you try anything once this is over, I won't hesitate to shoot,' Sean warned him.

Bloom laughed bitterly. 'Let's just see if any of us are left alive first.'

There was a tense wait that lasted over an hour. Then, the man Krebs had posted in the crumbling tower of the old monastery rang the rusty bell and they knew the enemy had arrived. A band of Apaches rode in on their swift horses armed with flaming torches which they hurled at the surrounding buildings, several of which burst into flames, but Krebs had planned his defences well and the hail of bullets which erupted drove the enemy back. Warriors tumbled from their mounts as they were hit, their torches falling harmlessly into the dust. Those behind them began an immediate retreat.

The general store was ablaze, however, and the man inside fell screaming through the window of the upper storey, his body engulfed in flames. Then he hit the ground with a sickening thud and lay still as the scent of scorched flesh rose into the air. The Apaches leading the attack had managed to reach the outer walls of the monastery before their companions retreated. One of them was dressed in a lieutenant's tunic, presumably taken from the unfortunate Morse.

The warrior wielded a rifle in one hand while guiding his horse with the other and shot the man Krebs had placed in the bell tower. The soldier's body landed with a gaping wound in the chest. The Apache's mount now leaped over the outer wall.

Sean hit him in the throat with a single shot and the horse reared as its rider fell back with a spurt of blood and a gurgled cry. The others dismounted and crept among the ruins, hoping to surround and kill them. A buckskin-clad warrior, his face smeared with war paint, leaped at Pedro who fired, hitting the man in the face. Munro dodged an arrow and shot two Apaches in quick succession as they leaped between the remains of buildings. Bloom fired blindly, quivering with fear, and then screamed as an arrow embedded itself in his leg. Carlos managed to hit the warrior shooting arrows at them from behind a crumbling pillar. The Apache staggered sideways as the bullet thudded into his shoulder and Chiquita finished him off as he lurched towards her. They were holding their own but it was a desperate fight and Sean was not convinced they would get out of the village alive.

6

Sean needed to reload and did so quickly but not quite fast enough. A bullet whizzed past his ear and he flung himself to the ground to find cover. It was Munro who came to the rescue, spinning in an arc to let off three bullets in rapid succession, all hitting their targets. There was expert aim and timing behind the shots and Sean watched in amazement as three warriors crumpled to the ground, each with a bullet straight through the heart.

There was a sudden lull in the fighting and Sean watched as Munro calmly began to reload.

'There's only one man I know who can shoot like that and he's supposed to be dead.'

'What are you talking about?' said Chiquita.

'Maybe you'd better ask him.' Sean gestured towards the silent Munro.

Munro's eyes met the girl's and he smiled sadly. 'I'm sorry, Chiquita, but I'm not the man you think I am. My name is George Munro, bank robber *extra-ordinaire*, gunfighter and identical twin of the late Father Joseph Munro.'

Pedro and Chiquita exchanged looks of astonishment as Munro went on to explain how he had taken refuge with his brother while suffering from fever following an escape from prison. The priest tended his wayward twin and the thief recovered only for Joseph Munro to succumb to the same illness.

'You took your brother's place, deceived the people of San Tomas and evaded justice,' said Sean. 'When this is over, I'm taking you back to prison where you belong.'

To his surprise, Munro took the news calmly. 'I expected as much. I knew what I was risking when I invited you to come to San Tomas.'

'It seems a strange way to repay a man for saving your life,' remarked Carlos.

'He was saving his own hide too,' replied Sean defensively.

'Really, Papa, how can you defend what this Munro has done?' demanded Chiquita.

Carlos sighed. 'When you have lived in the world as long as I have, my dear, you'll realize that there are many sides to all of us. Few people are entirely good or bad and I suspect that, given his conduct, Munro had some motivation beyond hiding from the law.'

'You are too soft-hearted,' Chiquita admonished him as she removed the arrow from Bloom's leg and bandaged the wound with a handkerchief.

'Perhaps, but I am also the coward who allowed Quinn to abuse his daughter. Now, here I am standing up to bandits and fighting Apaches. Sometimes, the greatest foe a man can conquer is his own weakness.'

They barely had time to reflect on these words before the sound of gunfire erupted once more as the Apaches returned for another attack. This time they tried a different tactic and kept their distance, firing a series of flaming arrows through the windows and on to the clapboard walls of the buildings before running for cover. By doing so, they obviously hoped to set the village ablaze and force their opponents out into the open. Sean could see that it was beginning to work as men emerged coughing and blinded by smoke into the street only to be cut down or shot by the Apaches.

'I suggest we counter-attack,' said Munro, as he rose to his feet.

The others followed, apart from the injured Bloom who remained behind to nurse his injured leg. They spread out cautiously as they advanced, firing at the Apaches from behind. The smoke billowing from the burning buildings provided some cover as they aimed shots at the attacking warriors. Clancy, the scar-faced deserter they had met earlier in the saloon, fired his pistol at an Apache only to hear the click of an empty chamber. Sean's first bullet caught the Indian between the shoulders and he fell dead in the act of raising his tomahawk to crush the renegade soldier's skull. Clancy shouted his thanks before diving for cover to reload. Munro shot down two more from their horses as they galloped towards him out of the smoke. Pedro joined Chavez and a few bandits as they formed a circle to fight off another group of mounted Apaches while the others headed for the cover of the dead blacksmith's forge.

Their assailants were slowly being driven back once more and several warriors had crouched down by the wagon Sean had purchased earlier. He strode out of the clouds of smoke, a gun blazing from each hand and watched as the painted warriors fell to the ground. Another leaped at him from the roof of the wagon as he turned away, but Carlos shot the man down and then marvelled at his sudden display of marksmanship.

'It just shows what you can do when

you try,' Sean told him with a grin.

Suddenly, all was quiet as the last shots were fired and the cries of dying men faded into silence. The remaining Apaches had retreated again and the defenders emerged from the cover of burnt out buildings to count their losses.

'Have they gone for good?' asked Chiquita nervously.

'You can never tell with Apaches,' replied Sean.

Chavez had lost five men and Krebs seven. A few others had suffered minor injuries. They stood cautiously in the street for a few minutes, waiting to see if the enemy would return. Just when they began to relax, however, Sean heard the sound of approaching hoofs and shouted at them to take cover. As the group scattered, a horse without a rider came galloping down the street with a cashbox tied to its tail. The lid had been opened and the paper money inside set alight. The Apaches may have been beaten but they had made sure the victors would not get the spoils.

One of the deserters broke from his cover with a howl of anguish and ran towards the horse in a vain attempt to salvage some of the box's contents. As he did so, an arrow sailed through the air and struck him between the shoulder blades. The others watched as he fell dead to the ground.

'Damned fool,' muttered Sean. 'That's exactly what they want us to do.'

The horse wheeled around again and Sean aimed at the rope binding its tail to the cashbox. With a single shot, the cord was broken and the poor animal ran off, freed at last from its burden. The remains of the payroll lay smouldering in the road, and the survivors emerged to gather round the scorched shreds of paper.

Krebs kicked over the burnt out cashbox with his boot and spat on the ashes with disgust.

'Goddamn it, there ain't nothin' I hate more than Apaches!'

'Hardly worth the lives of your

comrades, was it?' said Sean.

'We'd all be dead now if we'd stayed with the column,' replied Krebs in a sour tone.

'I guess we'd better rejoin our regiment,' suggested Clancy. 'There's no sense in desertion if we're just gonna be poor. Besides, we all got pay comin' to us and we can be heroes when we get back: the men who fought off the Apaches.'

Krebs shook his head. 'I ain't goin' back to listen to that damn drill sergeant yellin' orders. We won't be gettin' any medals or extra pay, anyhow.'

'You mean we should let 'em think we're dead and stay that way?' enquired Clancy.

'You can do what you like,' interrupted Sean. 'This is where we part company.'

'Not so fast,' said Chavez. 'I think maybe we could use these gringos. What do you say, Krebs?'

The deserter grinned. 'I always

fancied myself as an outlaw. Yeah, I reckon we could join up with you, Chavez.'

Clancy and the others murmured their assent before the former soldiers went off to search what was left of the village in an effort to find some civilian clothes. Sean went back to find Bloom, his companions following, but there was no sign of the injured traitor anywhere among the monastery ruins. He stood, looking around, swearing softly.

'He can't have got far,' said Pedro.

'We don't know that,' warned Munro. 'He probably stole a horse during the confusion and got away under the cover of all that smoke.'

'Damn it, that's all I need,' said Sean. 'Bloom is sure to warn Quinn and now I've got to watch my back against a bunch of thieves and cutthroats.'

'There are some you can rely on,' Pedro reminded him.

'One or two,' conceded Sean, though he did not look at Munro when he said it.

Chavez, Krebs and their combined forces climbed into the back of the wagon as they prepared to leave. The deserters were now clad in an assortment of ill-fitting civilian clothes they had looted from the village. Munro swung himself into his horse's saddle and announced that he was riding on ahead.

'Don't try to run out on me,' Sean warned him. 'I'll track you down no matter how long it takes.'

'I'm going after Bloom, but you just believe what you want,' said the fugitive, as he rode off.

Carlos watched him disappear in a cloud of dust. 'Perhaps he was telling you the truth, Marshal.'

Sean had always thought that the world was divided into those who were honest and those who were not, with men like Munro in the second category. He tended to be suspicious of criminals who had supposedly reformed, yet the fake priest's conduct did not make sense. Munro had placed himself at risk in order to help the people of San Tomas and had not abused the position his brother's death had given him. On the contrary, he seemed to have carried out his duties in an exemplary manner. Sean was perplexed by the man's motives but found it difficult to acknowledge the possibility that Munro was a changed man.

'The man's a thief and an imposter, that's all we know for certain.' Carlos did not answer while Chiquita chewed her lip thoughtfully. To hell with them, thought Sean. If they were fooled by Munro's antics then so be it. The villain was bound to show his true colours sooner or later.

Back in San Tomas, the gallows was almost built. Cartwright watched from the window of his cell as the finishing touches were added. One of Quinn's men, Todd Reynolds, sat on guard watching him and his companion, Garcia.

'You won't have much longer to wait,' Reynolds told them. 'The colonel plans to string you up before nightfall.'

'I wish Fr Munro was here with us,' sighed Garcia.

'Prayers won't save either of you,' jeered the guard.

'Can't you at least be quiet and just leave us alone?' asked Cartwright.'

Reynolds shrugged. 'Suit yourselves. Pass the time however you want.'

At that moment Quinn strode in and approached the barred door of the men's cell.

'What are you waiting for, Quinn? Why don't you just get on with it?' asked Cartwright bitterly.

'Be patient, all in good time,' said Quinn mockingly, as he glanced at his pocket watch. 'Bloom should be leading your friends into the little trap I've set for them. You wouldn't want to miss the fun, would you?'

'What have you done with Father Munro?' demanded Garcia.

'Your heroic little priest seems to have run away,' the colonel sneered.

'He'll be back with lots of help,' said

Garcia defiantly.

Quinn smiled as the sounds of sawing and hammering stopped. 'I wouldn't count on it, not in time to save you anyway.' He snapped the lid of his watch shut and put it away. 'In another few hours it will all be over. Then my men will strip this town of everything that's of value and we'll leave the place to rot alongside the corpses on that gallows out there.'

Cartwright watched Quinn's retreating back as the colonel left the jail. 'He's probably right,' the former mayor told his companion disconsolately.

Garcia shook his head. 'No, there's still a chance, I'm sure of it. Father Munro's a good man and he'd never abandon us.'

'I wish I could share your optimism, old friend,' replied Cartwright, as he glanced once more out of the window at the newly built gallows.

Meanwhile, Philip Bloom's painful injury had slowed him down and the horse he had stolen was not used to carrying such a heavy burden. He stopped for a moment to swig some water before wiping the sweat from his face. His mount snorted heavily and he patted the animal, reassuringly. Once he reached San Tomas, he hoped Quinn would pay him off in return for the vital information he was bringing and send him on his way with a fresh horse.

Suddenly, he heard cries coming from behind. A group of four Apaches was in pursuit, probably survivors from the battle. Cursing, he dug his spurs into his horse's flanks and set off once more at a gallop. Casting a nervous glance backwards, he saw that his pursuers were gaining on him. Bloom drew his revolver and fired several times but he was a poor shot and the Apaches weaved from side to side, easily dodging the bullets. Moments later a spear sailed passed his ear and he clung to his horse, whimpering with fear.

Suddenly he heard shots and crouched low before realizing that they had not been aimed at him. Bloom looked back once more, this time with relief, as two of his assailants tumbled from their mounts. The remaining warriors turned to face the attack and were each shot down by the dark-suited figure who was now galloping towards him at speed.

'Stay where you are, or you're a dead man!' shouted a familiar voice.

Bloom raised his hands in the air with a sigh of resignation. He knew better than to try to escape from Munro, having witnessed how well the man could shoot. Still, he supposed he was better off than he had been a few moments ago. The Apaches would probably have caught him and skinned him alive.

'It was lucky for you I showed up,' said Munro as he drew to a halt. 'Now, take your gun in your left hand and throw it away from you.'

Bloom obeyed wordlessly, all the time keeping his eyes on his captor who now gestured for him to dismount.

'Do you have to point that gun at me all the time? I know how fast you are,

I'm unarmed and my horse is worn out so I'm not going anywhere in a hurry.'

'I guess you're right,' said Munro, holstering his weapon. 'Now just take it easy while we wait for the others.' Both men got down from their mounts and Bloom noticed that one of the Apache horses had stopped nearby.

'I know you could outrun me on a fresh horse, but don't even think about it,' said Munro, shaking his head. 'You won't reach that animal before I plug you.'

Bloom shrugged. 'I guess not. Do you mind if I sit while we wait?'

Munro nodded and his prisoner slumped to the ground. Suddenly the would-be priest felt a stinging sensation as a fistful of sand caught him in the eyes, blinding him temporarily. His hands flew up to his face as Bloom made a grab for the dead Apache's horse. The animal was frightened by the sudden movement, however and bolted. Munro saw his assailant dimly through a blurred vision of tears. He leaped wildly at him and the two men tumbled to the ground in a sprawling heap. Bloom's plump figure squirmed desperately in a bid to escape, but Munro winded him with a blow to the stomach. The fat man now made a grab for his discarded gun which was lying nearby but felt the barrel of Munro's own weapon shoved under his chin.

'Keep still!' commanded Munro as he knelt astride his captive. Munro's vision had now cleared and he leaned over to pick up Bloom's gun with his left hand, still holding his own with his right. Then he brought the butt of the revolver crashing down on the troublesome prisoner's forehead and watched with satisfaction as Bloom lapsed into unconsciousness.

'There now,' he muttered. 'That ought to keep you quiet for a while.'

When Sean and his companions arrived Bloom was sitting up, his hands bound, with an egg-sized bump on his head.

'I had a little trouble with him,'

explained Munro.

'We saw some dead Apaches back there,' said Pedro.

'They were after Bloom, but he didn't show me much gratitude.'

Sean looked at the crumpled figure with contempt. 'Try to escape once more and I'll shoot you. Is that understood?'

Bloom shot him a look of hatred but nodded wordlessly as he was hauled to his feet. Munro cut his bonds and hustled him up to the front seat of the wagon where Chavez, who had been driving the vehicle, handed him the reins.

'Just remember, gringo, my gun will be pointed at your head so no tricks when we drive into town. Stay smart and you'll live longer.' The bandit leader then climbed into the back with his followers and they set off on the last leg of their journey to San Tomas.

'I can't figure you out, Munro,' said Sean, as the two men rode together. 'Your cover story's been blown so why not just head for the border?'

'I can't quite figure it myself.'

'Come on, what's the plan? Do you think you'll get a pardon in return for helping these folks?'

Munro sighed. 'There's no plan, Marshal. When I first took my brother's place it was a means to hide but then I found that people trusted me, depended on me, and that I had a chance to do some good for a change. I'd been the black sheep all my life, only ever thinking about myself. Suddenly, I began to see the world through Joseph's eyes, a world that has needs, a world in which there's a lot of pain.'

'People like you cause that pain,' Sean told him sharply.

'Do you think I don't know that? I could have left San Tomas any time in the six months before Quinn showed up but I stayed because I realized I had a lot of paying back to do and San Tomas seemed a good place to do it.'

'You're not a real priest though, are you? Don't people deserve better than to be treated as a salve for your conscience?'

Munro shook his head. 'It's not as simple as that. When Joseph died, the townspeople were left without anyone to marry them, baptize their children, comfort the sick and bury the dead. It was because of me that happened; he caught the fever keeping me alive. I always planned to move on when a new priest arrived, but then there was Quinn to deal with.'

Sean took in the outlaw's words slowly. 'I guess I was wrong, Munro. There's some good in you after all. When we get back to Yuma, I'll have a word with the authorities. Maybe you'll get a reduced sentence instead of an increased one for escaping.'

'Thanks, Marshal. I know it's not an easy thing for you to admit that and I appreciate it but let's just see if we all get out of this alive first.'

* * *

It was not long before San Tomas loomed into view and Bloom drove the wagon along the main street as he had been ordered. Quinn watched from his suite on the top floor of The Bad Angel as the vehicle reached the centre of town with Sean, Munro, Pedro, Chiquita and Carlos following behind. Bloom had done well since it appeared he had brought back the plunder the marshal and his friends had captured from Quinn's men. Why else would he be driving a wagon? Nevertheless, Quinn still had no intention of paying that weasel the reward he had promised.

The first shot was fired from the church tower and hit Bloom squarely in the chest. Clancy quickly shoved the body aside and climbed up to take the reins while Chavez pulled the covering away from the wagon so that his followers could fire back at the men lining the rooftops. He then squeezed in beside Clancy and killed the lookout in the tower with his first shot, watching with satisfaction as he fell to his death.

Quinn's men had not expected to meet with such resistance and now scrambled to lie flat as they came under fire from a hail of bullets. They managed to hit several of the bandits but the ex-Confederates were being killed in greater numbers, rolling off the rooftops as they were shot down. Sean and the others had dismounted by this time to take cover and the opportunity to pick them off had been missed when Chavez launched his attack. The marshal crouched down low behind the fountain and fired at an open doorway. One of Quinn's men fell through it and lay still on the ground. Someone took a shot at him from a window of the general store and it ricocheted off the edge of the fountain. He rolled aside, firing again and another adversary tumbled through the shattered glass to his death.

His companions had spread out to take cover, continuing to exchange fire with the men on the rooftops. Sean watched Chiquita and her father dive into a barn and was relieved to see that they were safe, for now at least. Clancy stopped the wagon and the men inside jumped out to hide behind it, firing as they did so. Pedro exchanged shots with a man hiding in a hayloft who then fell back with a bullet in his chest. As he did so, his own last shot ignited the hay and the building quickly burst into flames.

Suddenly, Munro was at Sean's elbow and gestured for him to look further up the street to where a gallows had been erected. Two prisoners with ropes around their necks were being guarded by a few of Quinn's men, but now an extraordinary thing happened. Townspeople emerged from their homes to join in the fight and were trying to free Cartwright and Garcia. The people of San Tomas were standing up for themselves!

7

'Come on, let's go help them,' urged Sean as he ran forward, Munro and Pedro at his heels. Todd Reynolds and his men were beating back the crowd with their superior firepower and a bespectacled storekeeper fell dead to the ground as a gaping red wound spread across the white apron covering his chest.

Reynolds made a grab for the lever that would release the trapdoor beneath Cartwright and Garcia's feet, but Sean's first bullet hit him in the back and he spun round. The second shot went straight through his heart and he rolled off the platform. Munro was at his side, both guns blazing and the bodies of the remaining soldiers jerked like marionettes under the hail of bullets. The people surged forward with Pedro in the lead, climbed on to the platform and began to untie the two captives.

Clouds of black smoke now billowed across the street from the hayloft and the fire had spread to the barn. Carlos and Chiquita stumbled out into the street, coughing and spluttering. Sean ran over and guided them both to shelter in a doorway. The sounds of gunfire echoed all around them as the battle raged between Quinn's men and the bandits who followed Chavez. Dead bodies littered the street, many of them in grey tunics, which suggested that Quinn was losing. It was far from over yet, however.

'Stay here where it's safe,' Sean urged Chiquita.

'I'll take care of her,' said Carlos, his eyes streaming from the smoke. 'Go, do what you must to free San Tomas.'

The marshal set off at a run towards the hotel, dodging bullets as he crossed the street. He glanced down as he reached the other side and saw Clancy grimacing with pain as he clutched a wounded shoulder, blood from the bullet wound seeping between his fingers. Sean felt a twinge of sympathy as he reached the injured man since he had fought well and was hardly the worst of comrades. He paused to draw out a handkerchief which he thrust under Clancy's tunic.

'There, that ought to help stop the bleeding.'

'Thanks, Marshal.' The deserter held up a pistol. 'Go on. I'll cover you.' Sean nodded his thanks and stepped up on to the veranda while Clancy exchanged fire with one of Quinn's men who had the marshal in his sights.

As he entered the wreckage of the saloon, Sean sensed a rapid movement to his left. He turned as a man rose up from behind the bar to take a shot at him but the bullet which struck down his adversary came from another's gun. Munro stood behind him, grinning.

'I saw you come in here by yourself and thought you could use some help. Clancy's still covering us outside.'

'Saving my life's becoming a habit of yours,' replied Sean.

Munro lifted the head of the dead man slumped across the bar and gave a puzzled frown. 'It's Krebs. Why was he shooting at you?'

'It's as if he was here on lookout, but for what?'

Munro gestured towards the staircase. 'I suggest we go find out.'

Meanwhile, upstairs Quinn had seen which way the tide was turning and decided it was time to bail out. He stuffed a wad of cash he kept hidden in case of emergencies, some valuables and a few items of clothing into a leather bag and then prepared to climb out through the window. Suddenly, the door splintered on its hinges as it was kicked in and Chavez stood facing him, thumbing back the hammer on the pistol he held in his huge fist.

'Don't be in such a hurry, Colonel Quinn. We haven't even been introduced yet.'

'Who the hell are you?'

'It is your old enemy, Chavez. We fought on opposite sides once, remember?'

'Of course, you led a whole regiment of peasants for Juarez. Is this your revenge?'

'Not quite. I know about the money and the deeds to lands you have bought in Louisiana, all kept in a bank in Austin.'

Quinn nodded eagerly. 'We could do a deal. Help me get out of here and we'll split everything straight down the middle.'

Chavez corrected him. 'That will be three ways: I have a partner on guard downstairs.'

At that moment a shot rang out and both men froze. Then there were footsteps hurrying up the staircase.

'Correction, I had a partner,' said Chavez calmly. 'I suggest we take the window but first, move the desk across the door.' The Mexican gestured with the revolver and his captive hurried to do as he was told. Then the bandit leader shoved Quinn out on to the roof and squeezed through behind him, his gun at the colonel's ribs. Chavez knew he could never get access to the funds held in the account without Quinn. He needed his former enemy more than the colonel needed him and he was not about to take any chances.

Sean reached the door to Quinn's room moments later. He saw that the lock was broken but something heavy prevented him from gaining entry to the room. Munro joined him and the two men pressed their weight against the obstruction. The door opened slowly as the desk moved across the floor but they entered to find no sign of Quinn and the room in disarray.

'Come on, he's making a run for it!' shouted Sean as he spotted the open window and climbed out on to the roof. Munro followed closely behind and both men turned to see two figures jumping from one building to another through the clouds of gun-smoke. Sean leaped agilely after them while Munro struggled to keep up, the older outlaw not being as fit as he once was.

As he drew closer, Sean saw that Chavez appeared to be running with Quinn rather than chasing him, an impression confirmed when the Mexican turned to open fire. The marshal crouched down as a bullet whizzed past his ear but the two men disappeared before he had time to shoot back. Then he looked down and saw the two men darting across the square below. Munro caught up, panting.

'It looks like they're heading towards the old mine.'

'They won't get away so easily, come on!' urged Sean.

They both climbed down and raced after the fugitives. As they did so, Carlos was guiding Chiquita, still suffering from the effects of the smoke, across to the fountain to get some water. Quinn stopped abruptly in mid stride, seeing the opportunity to take a hostage and reached out to seize the young woman.

'No!' shouted Carlos and fumbled for his weapon, but the colonel had already drawn the knife he kept hidden inside the top of his boot and the old man sank to the ground as the blade entered his heart. Chiquita flung herself across his body, weeping, as Quinn reached out to pull her to her feet.

'There's no time!' cried Chavez, turning once more to fire at their pursuers and Quinn reluctantly released the girl as the two men ran on towards the mine.

Chiquita turned a face streaming with tears towards him as Sean stopped by her side.

'Get after them! Avenge my father's murder!' she cried and he hurried away, Munro still following.

Chavez had earlier placed two horses inside the mine after slipping away from the battle for a few minutes. He urged Quinn to hurry as he untied them and then the two men made their way through the tunnel. Their pursuers were not far away and Quinn heard footsteps echoing behind them as they approached the exit.

'I've got an idea. Fire at the roof just before we get outside,' he urged his companion.

Chavez turned as the two men emerged into the sunlight and directed several shots above their heads. The noise reverberated around the confined space, shaking the fragile wooden beams which supported the roof of the tunnel. There was a creaking sound followed by a cascade of rocks which threw up clouds of dust. Sean came to a halt, his path now blocked by a heap of rubble. Munro pointed with alarm to another stream of dust and stones tumbling from the roof.

'Let's get out of here, the whole thing's about to cave in!' he cried as both men began to cough and splutter. They turned and stumbled back towards the entrance as each remaining wooden beam groaned and snapped, unleashing further falls of rock. They barely made it outside before the entire structure collapsed in on itself, then settled into a pile of broken slabs and splintered wood.

Munro bent down, panting with effort between bouts of coughing, his black suit shrouded in dust.

'Are you all right?' Sean asked.

'Sure, it's not the first time I almost got myself killed although robbing banks was easier.'

'Well, it won't be easy catching those two. I wonder why Chavez is helping Quinn.'

'If you want to know the answer, just follow the money.'

Sean slapped his forehead. 'Of course, Chavez wants to get his hands on those bank deposits! That means they'll be heading for Austin so we've a long ride ahead of us. Are you sure you're up to it?'

'Do you figure on just riding all the way there, trying to follow their tracks?' Munro shook his head, smiling.

'What's so funny? Do you have a better idea?'

'No wonder you never caught me,

Marshal. You've got to think the way a fugitive thinks. Unless there are wanted posters of you all over the place, when you're on the run you go by the quickest, easiest route. Sometimes a man who might be recognized easily will do that anyway, if he has a good disguise that is.'

Sean thought for a moment and then the answer suddenly came to him. 'I've got it! They'll head for San Antonio and take the stage. It's only eighteen hours to Austin from there.'

'If they ride hard they could make the one that leaves the day after tomorrow.'

'Then what are we waiting for? Let's head back into town and get some fresh horses.'

The battle was over by the time they got back. Quinn's few remaining men were being herded into the jail and Cartwright was making a speech to the assembled townspeople, standing on the gallows from which he had so nearly been hanged. Pedro was comforting Chiquita as she sat next to her father's body. They both looked up as Sean approached, Munro following.

'Quinn got away. Chavez is with him, he double-crossed us but we think we know where they're headed.'

Chiquita stood up and wiped her face. 'I'm coming with you.'

'It will be dangerous — ' Sean began.

'My father died defending me. This is the least I can do.' Her gaze was steady and her tone unwavering. There was clearly no point in arguing.

'I'll come as well.' said Pedro decisively. 'Four against two will give you a better chance.'

'Well, I guess we'd better get started,' said Sean. 'It will be getting dark in an hour and harder to pick up their trail.'

Cartwright limped over to them as they prepared to ride off. 'If you're going after Quinn, why not wait a while and we'll get a posse together?'

Sean shook his head. 'There'd be too many people and that would slow us down. Besides, we can't afford to lose any more time.'

The former mayor nodded. 'I guess you're right. It might be better with just a few people, anyhow. We don't want this thing turning into a lynch mob.'

'I wouldn't mind that,' said Chiquita bitterly.

'I'm sorry about your father. He was a brave man,' Cartwright told her.

She gave him a brief, wintry smile and then they headed off into the dusk as Cartwright watched them go. Garcia came and stood alongside him.

'I hope they kill that bastard when they catch up with him.'

'Revenge won't get San Tomas back on its feet, Alberto,' murmured his old friend.

When Sean picked up two sets of tracks in the twilight, it was clear that Munro had been right. Quinn and Chavez were heading towards San Antonio.

'We'll make camp soon,' he announced.

'They won't be making camp,' said Chiquita, irritably. 'I say we should press on after them.'

'No, Sean's right,' protested Pedro.

'We've more chance of catching them if we're rested and the horses will last longer.'

'That's easy for you to say. It wasn't your father who got killed!' she snapped.

'I know how hard this is for you, Chiquita, but we mustn't forget the most important reason for catching up with Quinn,' Munro urged her. 'We need to get back what he stole because the town's future depends on it.'

'Don't you think it's about time you quit preaching? We all know you're a thief yourself, not a priest like you pretended to be.'

Munro nodded. 'That's true and I know to my cost how killing, just like stealing, can be a hard habit to break. I once swore I'd never pick up a gun again but lately I've had to and so have you. You want to kill Quinn, I understand that, but don't let the desire to do it take over and rot your soul.'

'Like it rotted yours, you mean? Look, Munro, after I've put a bullet in

Quinn, I'll go back to being the same person I was before. I won't be turning into a criminal like you, OK?'

Munro shrugged. 'That's not what I meant but never mind. Just forget it.'

'Come on, let's stop arguing. There are some rocks further up so we'll camp there until first light,' said Sean. He, too, was concerned about Chiquita and how grief and rage were clouding her judgement. Still, it was only natural and there was little he could do about it apart from trying to keep her in check.

Chiquita remained cold and distant in her manner while they ate supper and took up a position well away from her companions when they settled down for the night. Sean was troubled by her attitude but too tired to give the problem much thought and soon drifted off into a dreamless slumber.

His awakening the next morning was an abrupt one. Munro was shaking him roughly and speaking with some urgency.

'For God's sake, what is it?' Sean asked.

'It's Chiquita. She's gone.'

He sat up abruptly and looked around him. He saw with alarm that her horse and bedroll had also disappeared.

'She must have left during the night,' added Pedro.

Sean threw his blanket aside and started to pull on his boots. 'I just hope we catch up with her before she catches up with Quinn and Chavez.'

Chiquita had lain awake fuming for two hours the previous night. How dare the high and mighty marshal stop her from going after her father's killer? As for that lying thief, Munro, she had no intention of listening to him! Pedro had also disappointed her and she pitied poor Maria for having a man with iced water in his veins for a husband. Then, when she heard the others snoring, the idea that she should just get up and leave occurred to her. She had more reason to hate Quinn than any of them and if they were not men enough to do a man's job then she would just have to do it herself. Creeping away had been surprisingly easy and, as she rode off into the night, Chiquita felt confident that Silas Quinn would be dead by morning.

Meanwhile, Chavez was making sure that Quinn rode in front of him all the way to San Antonio and kept a pistol pointed at the former colonel's back at all times. He had removed the American's gunbelt but, even so, he was taking no chances. For his part, Quinn was tired of this unwanted companion. At best, he stood to lose half his money if he failed to rid himself of the Mexican before reaching the bank in Austin. He shuddered when he considered the worst that could happen. Quinn did not trust Chavez to keep to his end of the deal. There was something in the man's eyes, a flicker of hatred that emerged when the southerner turned to speak to him which suggested otherwise. Fortunately, the Mexican had not searched him for concealed weapons and Quinn still had the derringer he always kept hidden in his pocket. All he needed was the chance to use it.

'You won't be able to keep this up when we hit town. People will ask questions, especially on the stage.'

Chavez responded with a deep chuckle. 'I'm smarter than you think, gringo. We will be handcuffed together and you will have a pistol pointed at me, an empty one, of course. I will have the loaded one hidden inside my jacket. You're going to wear a silver badge and pretend to be taking this bad old bandit to prison in Austin.'

'Very clever,' conceded Quinn. 'What happens when we get to the bank?'

'The handcuffs come off but I'll still have the loaded gun. Just hand over my half of the money and there'll be no trouble, OK?'

'You won't get a cent if you shoot me. Those funds can't be released without me being there in person to sign for them.'

'You can still sign with a bullet in

each leg, don't forget that,' Chavez warned him. 'OK, we've come far enough. We'll sleep a few hours until daylight.'

The two men dismounted in the moonlight and the Mexican gestured for Quinn to sit with his back against a nearby tree. The former colonel suddenly found himself stunned as Chavez clubbed him with the butt of his pistol and then swiftly bound him with a rope.

'There, that should keep you quiet for the night,' he said with evident satisfaction.

As dawn broke, Chiquita watched from behind a sheltered outcrop of rock as Chavez rose and kicked the dying embers of the fire. She saw him look around, glance at the sleeping, bound figure of Quinn and squint up at the higher branches of the tree. He could not reach them and she watched as the bandit set off to find some firewood, grumbling to himself as he did so. Creeping out from behind her hiding place, Chiquita approached the tree, a revolver clutched in her hand. She kicked Quinn's foot to wake him and a sleepy eye opened slowly, then widened in alarm.

'If you call out for Chavez I'll blow your head off right now,' she warned him.

'You really shouldn't do that, my dear. I can make you rich, richer than you've ever dreamed of being,' he whispered.

Chiquita shook her head and thumbed back the hammer on the pistol. 'I don't want a cent of your stinking money, I just want you dead. You killed my father and now you're going to pay.'

Quinn swallowed hard as a sudden realization chilled his bones. No amount of avarice could overcome this woman's desire for revenge.

'Your papa had a gun and he was trying to shoot me. I didn't want to kill him,' he protested lamely.

'Have you got any more last words before I send you to Hell?' she asked coldly.

Quinn tried desperately to think of some means of delaying her. 'I . . . I . . . have a last request. Just let me say my prayers, make my peace with God before it's too late,' he pleaded.

Chiquita hesitated, unsure of how to respond as the colonel shut his eyes and began to recite a litany of childhood prayers. All the while he was wriggling his hands free from the rope which bound him, hoping to reach the derringer in his pocket before it was too late.

'That's enough,' she told him abruptly. Quinn opened his eyes and she aimed the pistol at his head. Chiquita prepared to squeeze the trigger as her enemy stared back, his gaze transfixed by terror. Somehow, despite all her hatred of him, she found it difficult to fire. Shooting a man in cold blood, even Silas Quinn, was proving to be a lot harder than she had expected.

Sensing her hesitation, he began to speak once more. 'I don't blame you for wanting to put an end to me. I've done you more than enough harm, but I didn't shoot your papa in cold blood, tied up like this. I'm a soldier, I never — '

'Shut up!' she hissed at him. 'You're going to die and that's the end of it.' Chiquita steadied her aim and tried once more to stiffen her resolve.

'Drop the gun, *señorita*. It would be a shame to shoot a beautiful lady like you.'

Chavez had returned and she heard a menacing click as he cocked his weapon. Reluctantly, she lowered the pistol and tossed it to one side. She felt a hand on her shoulder as the bandit turned her around to face him, then stroked her cheek with the barrel of his gun.

'You came after him for revenge, eh? You're quite a woman, I must say.'

'Save your soft words for the whores who want to hear them,' she said coldly.

Chavez laughed loudly. 'Maybe you'll change your mind when you see me rich.'

'He told me about the money, trying

to save his miserable neck,' said Chiquita contemptuously.

Chavez gestured towards the bundle of sticks he had gathered for firewood and she bent down to start the fire. Then he crouched beside her and began whispering in Spanish. Chiquita listened wordlessly as he outlined his plan.

8

Two hours later, Sean was crouching by the remains of the fire as Munro examined the surrounding tracks.

'There are three sets of hoofmarks leading away from here. It looks like they've got her, I'm afraid.'

'I can't see any signs of a struggle,' said Pedro, frowning. 'It seems to me that she went with them willingly.'

Sean looked up sharply. 'How can you say that?'

Pedro shrugged. 'I've known Chiquita a long time but she hasn't been herself lately.'

'How would you be if your father had just been murdered?' demanded Sean hotly.

'Well, if she did go willingly, she must have had a good reason,' said Munro, soothingly. 'We all know why she came after them alone in the first place.'

Sean rose from his haunches and got back on to his horse. 'I reckon that puts her in danger and we won't catch up if we stand around here jawing all day. Come on, let's go.'

They set off once more, setting a steady pace as the landscape slowly changed. They emerged from the edge of the desert to cross a rocky escarpment before reaching a savannah of short grasses, shrubs and trees. San Antonio, its long winding river and the road to Austin was still a long ride ahead of them. It was a hot day and Sean stopped to wipe the sweat from his face. He looked up and saw three tiny figures on horseback in the distance.

'Hey, I think that could be them.'

'It is,' said Munro. 'They'll ride until after sunset and set off again at first light. That way they can reach San Antonio before the eight o'clock stage leaves tomorrow.'

'Then we'll do the same,' said Sean with grim determination. 'I don't plan on trailing behind all the way to Austin.'

'Then I hope you've worked a plan out about what to do once we catch up with them because I haven't.'

'I've got a plan, all right, don't you worry,' Sean assured him.

Up ahead of them, Chiquita was thinking about what Chavez had told her that morning.

'Listen, I have just as much reason to hate this gringo as you,' he had begun in a conspiratorial whisper.

'Then why help him to escape?' she had asked suspiciously.

'It's all part of my revenge. I'm going to steal his money and then kill him.'

'Why do you want to kill him?'

'You know that I fought for Juarez, alongside your friend Pedro and that Quinn was on the side of Maximilian?'

She frowned. 'So, that war's over now. What about it?'

'I never told Pedro this, it is a secret I carry with me.' From inside his jacket Chavez drew out a faded sepia photograph which was badly singed around the edges, showing a young couple with a small child. 'That was my sister, her husband and their young son, my nephew. They lived in one of the villages Quinn burned during the war and they died, screaming in flames while he watched.'

'How do you know it was him?'

'One man survived because he was able to hide. He came to join my men and he brought me this photograph, all that was left in their home.'

'What do you want me to do?' she asked.

'Nothing, act as if you're just my prisoner but give no trouble. I will kill Quinn for us both and then let you go, if that is what you want, or you can stay with me and help spend his money. The choice is yours.'

'Just kill him, that's all I want,' she told him.

Chavez nodded wordlessly and rose to his feet. Then, for Quinn's benefit he had waved his gun around and shouted at her to hurry up. 'Come on, woman, make coffee quickly. We must go soon!'

Now the bandit's apparent act of altruism in coming to the rescue of San Tomas made perfect sense. Greed played a part, but that too was linked to a desire for revenge. Chavez would relish depriving Quinn of his ill-gotten gains, seeing the look of fear in his eyes and hearing him beg for his life before he killed him. However, though Chiquita wanted her father's killer dead, she was no longer sure that it would give her the sort of satisfaction it was going to give Chavez.

Quinn was riding in front, Chavez pointing a gun at his back while Chiquita remained at the bandit's side, hands bound to the saddle in front of her.

'Why did you bring her with us? She makes me nervous,' complained Quinn.

Chavez winked at her as he replied, 'Oh, she's too pretty to leave behind. When I have all that money to spend, she'll be happy to be my woman.'

'I wouldn't count on it,' the former colonel warned him. 'She's likely to stab you in your sleep and I don't want her following me when our business is done.'

'You worry too much, *amigo*,' said Chavez, laughing.

Quinn was worried. Apart from not wanting to share his money with the bandit, he still harboured a nagging suspicion that Chavez did not intend him to leave Austin alive. The derringer was still safe in his pocket but now there were two of them to take care of. There was also the question of why the girl had been alone. He had expected the interfering marshal or a posse of some sort, but not just her. It did not make sense.

'Don't you think it strange that she's come after us all by herself? Where are the others?'

'What others?'

'Don't you think the people of San Tomas want their money back and to see me punished? What's Barry doing?'

Chavez turned and looked suspiciously at Chiquita. 'Now I come to think of it,

Quinn's right. So, maybe you'd better tell me who else is following us.'

'I don't know. I came after him for my own reasons.' Chiquita had been angry with Sean but she had no wish to place him or the others in danger. In fact, she would be perfectly happy to see them ride up and capture Quinn right now. The wretch would hang for what he had done, Chavez could still get justice and the townspeople would get their money back.

'Don't lie to me, Chiquita, or I might have to change my plans for you completely.' There was a hard edge to the bandit's tone and it was clear that he meant what he said. 'Maybe you'll talk better if I put a bullet in your leg,' he added.

'I can't tell you what I don't know,' she insisted defiantly.

Chavez fired a bullet just in front of her horse and the animal reared in fright. 'The next one's for you,' he told her.

'All right, I'll tell you. Sean Barry,

Munro and Pedro are following. I left them last night because I thought they were too slow and that Quinn was going to get away.'

The bandit's smile returned with a flash of gold teeth. 'That wasn't so hard, was it?'

'Maybe you'd better give me a gun,' said Quinn, hopefully.

'They haven't caught up yet so go a little faster and maybe they won't. We'll be safe once we're on that stage.'

Meanwhile, Sean and his companions were gradually closing the gap between them and their quarry. As they did so, however, it became more difficult to keep out of sight and when Chavez took a backward glance across the savannah, he spotted the three figures riding behind them in the distance.

'We've got company,' he remarked.

Quinn turned around in the saddle. 'I can just about see them. It must be Barry and his friends. They're still a fair way behind so maybe we can outrun them.'

Chavez shook his head. 'There's a clump of trees in a gully up ahead so we'll make for that and wait. I'll pick them off with my rifle once they get within range.'

Quinn spurred his horse and galloped towards the sheltered spot, the others following behind.

'How can you think of killing those men? Only yesterday you were fighting alongside them!' protested Chiquita.

The bandit shrugged. 'Sometimes yesterday's friend is today's enemy. They're after the money, same as me.'

'What would your sister and her family say if they were here? Would they want you to kill those who are also trying to avenge Quinn's victims?'

'They're dead. How do I know what they'd say?' he replied roughly as they followed Quinn into the gully.

Once they were all hidden, Chavez drew out his rifle and squinted along the barrel through a gap in the foliage. He waited for their pursuers to draw near. Quinn drew in just behind and surreptitiously felt for the derringer in his pocket, holding the reins with his left hand. Once the bandit had taken care of the opposition, a single bullet fired at close range would finish him off too. The girl was tied up and had no weapon so he did not need to worry about her.

As Chavez prepared to take aim, however, Chiquita's words returned to haunt him. He could imagine only too clearly what they would say; that he was dishonouring their memories and placing his own greed above justice. He lowered the rifle and turned to face the colonel, drawing the picture from inside his jacket as he did so.

'What are you doing? They'll be within range in a minute!' protested Quinn incredulously.

'I don't give a damn! Just look at this picture!' bellowed Chavez.

Quinn glanced at the faded photograph and looked up in confusion. 'What the hell has that got to do with anything?'

The bandit leaned forward and thrust the picture in front of his enemy's face. 'Look at it! See the faces of the people you killed!'

'I don't know what you're raving on about! Shoot that marshal, for God's sake!' The former colonel was panicking now as the sound of galloping hoofs drew nearer. Chavez dropped the rifle and grabbed Quinn by the lapels, almost pulling him from his horse as he drew him nearer.

'You killed my sister Juanita, her husband Eduardo and their son Hector when you burned their village! I don't give a damn about your stinking money so long as I — '

The muffled shot from the derringer pressed against his chest cut off the Mexican's last words and he slumped from his horse to the ground, Quinn prising the dead man's fingers away from his jacket. Chiquita looked down at the bandit's eyes widened in shock and rage at the moment of death and let out a scream of horror.

Quinn bent down and scooped up the rifle before turning to take aim at his pursuers. It took him a moment to realize that they were no longer there. He could not see or even hear any sign of them. Cursing, he turned his attention to Chiquita and rammed the muzzle of the rifle under her chin.

'You'd better show yourselves and drop your weapons, all three of you, or the girl dies!' he cried.

'All right, we're coming out with our hands up!' called Munro from the edge of the gully. Two figures emerged from the trees on foot, their hands in the air.

'Where's the marshal?' demanded Quinn suspiciously as he pointed the rifle at Pedro and Munro. It was the moment Sean had been waiting for and he leaped from his hiding place in the branches above, crashing into the body of his foe. Both men hit the ground in a sprawling heap, the marshal jerking the barrel of the rifle upwards so that it fired harmlessly into the air.

Pedro and Munro now piled in,

hauling Quinn to his feet as Sean finally gained possession of the rifle.

'It looks like we'll all be going to Austin together,' the marshal told their scowling prisoner. Pedro went over and untied Chiquita's hands while she wept with relief.

'I'm sorry for what I did, running off like that,' she told them all.

'Forget it, everything's fine now,' Munro assured her.

'I wouldn't count on that,' Quinn sneered. 'I won't sign for that deposit box in Morgan's Bank and you won't get a cent back unless I do.'

'A judge can order the bank to release it which he will when he hears our evidence,' said Sean.

Quinn threw back his head and laughed. 'Do you think the bank won't contest that? They'll hire lawyers and keep the thing tied up for years. Half what's in there will get spent in fees!'

'You could make it easy on yourself by co-operating,' said Sean.

The former colonel shook his head

vehemently. 'No, I'm bound to hang if we do everything legally. The only way you'll get that money is if I choose to let you have it, which I'll only do if you give me a solemn promise, on your word of honour, to let me go free afterwards.'

Quinn was looking straight into Sean's eyes as he said these words. He knew that the marshal was the sort of man who would abide by any deal he made, however distasteful it might be.

'You must be crazy, there's no way I'm going to do that,' he told him contemptuously.

Pedro drew out a long sharp knife and lightly scraped the blade down Quinn's cheek, just grazing the skin. 'Maybe there are some things we could try that might persuade you to do what's right,' he said.

'Do your worst,' said Quinn defiantly. 'It's my freedom in exchange for the money and that's the only deal I'll make. Torture me and the bank will get suspicious. The box won't be opened if

I seem under duress.'

'You seem pretty confident about what the bank will and won't do,' remarked Munro.

'Andrew Morgan owns that bank and he served under my command in the war. He was a fine officer then and he's a damned good banker now, one who knows how to look after his clients' interests.'

'We don't have to make a decision about this now,' said Sean. 'Let's leave it until we get to Austin.' He picked up the rifle which had belonged to the unfortunate Chavez and tossed it to Pedro. 'Here, you can help keep an eye on Quinn, but don't kill him unless you have to.'

They buried Chavez and then set off again, wisely ordering their prisoner to ride in front with Pedro's rifle at his back. Quinn's mind worked feverishly as he tried to work out a solution to his predicament. He was now in a worse situation than before, with three hostile companions who were unlikely to let him go, even if he gave back what he had stolen.

'There's enough money and land deeds in that deposit box to make more than just one of us very rich indeed,' he remarked as Pedro rode behind him.

'Forget it, everything in there's going back to the people you robbed — which includes me, by the way.'

'Don't you feel entitled to a bigger share? You did more than most of those townspeople to get rid of my men.'

Pedro shrugged. 'I just want what was stolen from me, not what belongs to anybody else.'

'If it wasn't for you they wouldn't be getting anything back. Listen, we could team up, leave the others behind and collect half the money. The rest can be sent to San Tomas if you want.'

Pedro shook his head. 'You disgust me, Quinn. You think that everyone else is like you, only out for themselves.'

'We could take just a quarter of the money. There, that would be fairer and you'd have a clear conscience.'

'Sean and the others would come after us. I'd have to shoot at them and where would my clear conscience be after that? No, you can keep riding and stay quiet from now on. I don't want to listen to any more of your schemes.'

Quinn rode on, cursing himself. He had overplayed his hand and put the Mexican on guard into the bargain. It was a shame he did not have Munro behind him. The bank robber turned fake priest might choose to abandon his pious act when faced with the same offer. Quinn decided to look for an opportunity to talk to him before they reached Austin.

The heat of the afternoon gave way to a cool sunset as they made their way across the savannah. As the orange light dimmed, Sean called them to a halt and they made camp. Munro approached Pedro and took the rifle from him, offering to watch their prisoner for a while.

'You might find that he talks too much,' the Mexican warned as he turned to walk away.

‘A man with high ideals,’ remarked Quinn, as he watched Pedro’s retreating back. ‘We’re a different breed altogether, having been on both sides of the law,’ he added shiftily.

‘Speak for yourself,’ said Munro, gesturing for the former colonel to sit down.

‘You can’t fool me with this act of yours, or our heroic marshal either. He’s going to clap you in chains and take you back to Yuma.’

‘Don’t tell me: you’ve got a much better idea,’ said Munro sarcastically.

Quinn started outlining a plan for them to make a run for it during the night and split the proceeds of the deposit box between them when they reached Austin. ‘If we leave them with no horses, they’ll never catch up. Then you can cross the border as a wealthy man,’ he added.

Munro shook his head. ‘I was a thief once, Quinn, but no longer. I don’t expect you to understand why so just forget it.’

The former colonel lapsed into silence, finally realizing that he was not going to make any allies in his plans for escape. Once the camp-fire was burning, he was given a plate of beans and some hot coffee in a tin cup. Quinn sat spooning the food into his mouth and then had a sudden thought as he raised the steaming cup to his lips. A flick of the wrist was all it took for the hot liquid to land in Munro's face and he followed up with a grab for the rifle. Munro roared in pain but did not release his weapon and the gun went off with a loud crack as the two men engaged in a tug of war.

Quinn was thrown backwards by the force of the blast from a shot fired at such close quarters. Blood flowed from his mouth and the scorched wound on his chest while Munro cursed as he stood up, blinking through the tears from his scalded eyes. The others gathered around and looked down at the crumpled body.

'Well, I guess we might as well turn back in the morning,' said Sean reluctantly. 'We won't be able to walk into that bank and get Quinn's deposit box just by asking for it.'

'No, not by asking for it,' agreed Munro, as he wiped his eyes with a handkerchief 'but that doesn't mean we should turn back.'

'What do you mean?' asked Pedro.

'I mean that it's time for me to resurrect my old skills. I've robbed banks before and I'm sure this one will be no different. It will have its weak points like all the rest.'

Sean shook his head. 'We can't put one crime right by committing another. There are times when the law doesn't seem fair, but it's still the law.'

'I'm only talking about that one deposit box. There's no need to take anything else.'

'You can't just go in and take it. There are legal processes to go through — '

'Yes, and you heard what Quinn had to say about all that!' Munro cut in. 'He made it obvious that his old pal Morgan, the one who owns the bank, is a crook who'll use every legal trick there is to stop that money going back to its rightful owners. Now that may be the law, Sean, but is it justice?'

'I don't think it is,' said Chiquita.

'I agree,' added Pedro. 'Sometimes you have to bend the law to do what's right.'

'I still don't like it,' said Sean. 'If you rob a bank you have to use guns, and if you use guns people might get hurt.'

'I can work out a plan that doesn't involve a hold up. What about that?'

'I guess that might be our best option,' conceded Sean. 'Now, help me bury Quinn and then we'd all better get some sleep.'

9

They rose before dawn and rode off as the first streaks of red appeared in the sky. The rest of their journey was uneventful and their horses splashed across the San Pedro creek where it joined the San Antonio River. The cool of the early morning was giving way to the heat of the day as they entered the town, then rode across one of the many plazas, past the courthouse and the church of San Fernando.

The coach, owned by the stage company Risher & Hall, was not full and they were able to buy tickets to sit inside on their journey along the old San Antonio road to Austin. It was a long, bumpy ride and hot inside the coach with dust blowing in through the open windows but at least there were some stops along the way. They were able to get a late breakfast at Manacha

Spring where the stage stopped at a large, well-constructed house standing in a thick grove. They picked up more passengers at New Braunfels, a town with a large population of German immigrants. They then passed through San Marcos and finally reached their destination at midnight before sinking exhausted into bed at the first hotel they came to.

Sunlight filtered through the curtains the next morning as Sean awoke, stretching his limbs on the narrow bed. He ordered a bath and had his clothes cleaned while he enjoyed a long soak in the tub. By the time he came downstairs into the hotel's reception area, it was late morning and he looked around for his companions.

'I was wondering when you'd show up.'

Sean turned to his right as a man in a smart grey suit and derby hat lowered his newspaper to speak to him. It took the marshal a moment to recognize a clean shaven Munro who now wore steel-framed spectacles and sported a flower in his buttonhole, lending him an air of gentlemanly sophistication.

'What's all this?' he asked.

Munro drew a business card from his waistcoat pocket and handed it over. 'I had it made at a print shop this morning while I was out getting this suit and seeing a barber,' he explained.

Sean looked at the false name, Rufus Bell and the string of letters after it implying the possession of a law degree and other qualifications.

'I don't get it. What do you hope to achieve with all this?'

'You're talking to Silas Quinn's legal representative, a status that has got me a private meeting with Mr Morgan this afternoon.'

'What do you want me to do?' Sean asked.

'Let's take a walk.'

As the two men set off along the street, Munro drew out a wad of cash from inside his jacket, peeled off some bills and handed them to him. 'Quinn had this on him when we buried him, his emergency fund. I want you to buy us some horses,' he whispered conspiratorially.

'It sounds like you've got everything figured out.'

'Turn right here,' said Munro, as they reached a corner. About halfway along the next street, he stopped outside a building constructed in the Spanish colonial style and pointed to the words above the door: Morgan's Bank. 'Be at the back of that building with the others at two o'clock, ready to ride out of town.'

'I just hope you know what you're doing,' said Sean.

Munro grinned. 'Don't worry. I'll keep you out of jail.'

That afternoon, Andrew Morgan eased his bulky frame back into the plush leather chair behind his desk after shaking hands with the man who introduced himself as Rufus Bell. The banker frowned as he glanced once more at the business card that had been presented to him before handing it back.

'Colonel Quinn writes to me with instructions from time to time. He never said anything about hiring a lawyer.'

'Well, he's a busy man as you know and doesn't have the time to check up on things, which is why he chose just recently to retain my services.'

'What is it you're here to check up on?' asked Morgan suspiciously.

'I'm on my way down to Louisiana to inspect the land purchases you've made on the colonel's behalf,' replied Munro smoothly. 'I just need to see the deeds and to make sure I've got all the details right, and to deliver your bonus payment, of course.'

Morgan's hard grey eyes, deep set in his bullish features, suddenly lit up. 'What bonus payment?'

'Oh, didn't my client tell you?' asked Munro in mock surprise. 'He's so pleased with your work that he's authorized me to give you an additional payment of a thousand dollars on top of your commission.'

Morgan watched as his visitor drew out a bundle of cash and placed it on the desk between them.

'Well, Mr Bell, I think that this calls for a drink.'

'I'll have one later, perhaps, when we've concluded our business. I assume you've had the deposit box sent up?'

Morgan rose from his chair and went over to a large safe in a corner of the office. 'I had it sent up this morning,' he announced, suddenly eager to please. He then unlocked the safe and removed an iron box which he brought over to the desk.

'I sold all the jewels and other valuables the colonel sent as instructed. Recently, I made a further purchase of land which has increased the colonel's holdings considerably. He also has twenty thousand dollars left in cash.'

'Well done. Let's have a look at this land you've bought for him.'

Morgan spread out the deeds on the

desk and made a sweeping gesture with his large hands. 'Since the end of the war and the freeing of all the slaves, the price of property in the South has fallen considerably. I arranged the purchase of several adjoining plantations at auction. The colonel could raise a large crop, growing either tobacco or cotton, and with cash to invest . . . '

Morgan had not noticed Munro step behind him and the handkerchief soaked in chloroform that was suddenly clamped over his nose and mouth came as a complete surprise. No-one could hear the banker's muffled cries and his considerable strength was of no avail once he had breathed in the powerful drug. His limbs grew heavy as blackness descended and Munro staggered under the man's bulk. He quickly lowered the unconscious Morgan into his chair and emptied the deeds and the cash from the deposit box into a leather bag. Finally, he turned the key in the door to Morgan's office before pocketing it, then went to the window.

Sean, Pedro and Chiquita were waiting anxiously in the street below and he tossed the bag down to them. Sean caught it and then Munro climbed out on to the ledge. He gestured for Pedro to get a horse in position for him and then leaped nimbly into the saddle.

'It's a long time since I did that and I wasn't sure if I still could,' Munro told them as they galloped away through the streets of Austin. Soon they were clear of the town and back on the road to San Antonio.

'We did it!' whooped Pedro with delight.

'Not quite,' replied Munro, as he signalled for them all to halt. 'Morgan's going to want that money back when he wakes up so I'd better make Rufus Bell vanish pretty quick. Hand me that leather bag, there's another change of clothes in it.'

Sean tossed the bag over and Munro dismounted before disappearing behind some rocks. He emerged a few minutes later, minus his spectacles and dressed casually. As he put on a leather vest over his cotton shirt and tied a bandanna around his neck, Munro appeared to be just another traveller.

'Morgan will be looking for a smartly dressed swindler who travels alone,' he told the others as he set fire to the discarded clothes. 'This should keep him off the scent.'

'New Braunfels is on the way back home and we could reach it by tomorrow night. Why not skirt around San Marcos, which is a little too close for comfort, hide out in New Braunfels and catch the stage back to San Antonio the next day?' asked Sean.

'You're starting to think like me,' said Munro with a grin. 'It's the quickest way back and not what Morgan will expect. He'll assume I've headed straight for Mexico, avoiding towns so he'll go tearing around the borderlands looking for me.'

Chiquita shook her head. 'Silas Quinn was smart, whatever else he was, and he wouldn't have trusted this banker if Morgan was the sort of man who makes too many assumptions. Maybe we should put as much distance between him and ourselves as possible.'

Munro climbed back into the saddle. 'He won't be looking for us but somebody wearing spectacles and dressed in a grey suit. Besides, I gave him enough chloroform to keep him unconscious for a few hours.'

'I think you're right,' agreed Sean. 'Come on, let's head for that town.'

Chiquita shrugged but said nothing. Perhaps she just worried too much but instinct told her that the chance they were taking was one they might regret later.

Back in Austin, Andrew Morgan was stirring a lot sooner than Munro had anticipated. He was a big man and the amount of chloroform he had received was not a large dose for someone of his size. Had he been having an operation, it is likely that he would have awoken screaming in the middle of it. Fortunately for the banker, he experienced nothing worse than drowsiness as he came to.

Morgan shook his head to clear the fog from his mind and the room swam into focus as he rubbed his eyes. For a few moments, he struggled to recall what had happened until he noticed the empty deposit box on his desk. He looked around the room but it appeared that nothing else had been taken and the safe in the corner was untouched. Stumbling to his feet, he went over to the door but it was locked. Immediately he began to hammer on it, bellowing for someone to come with a spare key. Moments later the door was unlocked and a nervous-looking clerk stood on the threshold.

'What seems to be the trouble, Mr Morgan?'

'I've been robbed, damn it! The bastard got away with the entire contents of a deposit box!'

'I'll get the sheriff right away.'

Morgan seized the man's arm as he scurried off. 'No, I want this handled quietly, with discretion. Publicity about things being stolen wouldn't inspire confidence in our customers. Get me Blake Finch!'

The clerk hurried to do as he was told and Morgan sat down again behind his desk. Until a bullet in the leg left him with a limp and forced his premature retirement, Blake Finch had been the best and most ruthless bounty hunter in the business. Now he owned a livery in town but was still capable of going after a man and tracking him, at least for a few days and was willing to do so if the price was right. He was also willing to kill, even if the price on a man's head had not been set by the law, which suited Morgan's purpose just fine.

Finch arrived just minutes later with his spare frame clothed in a long, black coat. Morgan looked into a weather-beaten face, the dark eyes set deep like two holes scorched in desert sand. There was no pity in them, no feeling at all in fact, and though the banker was a hard man, he shivered inwardly.

'Is there somethin' I can do for you, Mr Morgan?' enquired Finch, in that flat monotone of his.

Morgan briefly explained what had happened that afternoon while the bounty hunter listened carefully.

'Are you sure what was in that box is all that he took?' asked Finch.

'I'm positive. Now, let's get down to business. I'm willing to pay five hundred dollars for the return of the contents of that box and the death of the man who stole from me. Are those terms acceptable to you?'

'Yeah, but I'll need a list of what was in that box so I'll know if it's all there. It might take some persuasion to find out where any missin' items might be, afore I shoot the man, that is. The job could take longer if that's how it turns out.'

Finch made this suggestion of torture in the same matter of fact tone with which he discussed all the other details. This was a man completely indifferent to human suffering, one who might even enjoy hurting others.

'That won't be necessary,' said Morgan, rising from behind his desk to buckle on a gunbelt. 'I'm coming with you. I want to see this fake lawyer get what's coming to him.'

Finch did not reply for he was already at the window looking down at the street below, a quiet area since Morgan's office faced out from the rear of the building. There were not many passers-by and with luck, he might pick up the fugitive's trail from there.

Soon the two men were mounted on horses and ready to set off as the bounty hunter peered thoughtfully at the hoofprints in the dusty road.

'The man we're lookin' for had help. I'd say there's four of 'em altogether.'

'How can you tell?' asked Morgan. 'Other people might have been past.'

'There's one set of prints deeper than the others as if a man landed heavily on a horse. He'd do that if he jumped from the window which he must have done on account of the door bein' locked from inside. There are three other sets beside it and they all lead off in the same direction, like they'd been here waitin' for somebody.'

'Maybe I should get some more men,' suggested Morgan.

The bounty hunter shook his head and spat out some chewed tobacco on the ground. 'No time, Mr Morgan. Besides, I've taken care o' more men than that.' Then he led the way briskly out of town.

They were some miles away when Finch raised his hand and stopped suddenly, sniffing the air. He dismounted as Morgan drew in behind him and began poking the ground near some rocks with a stick.

'What is it?' asked the banker impatiently.

'Somebody's been burnin' stuff here, looks like clothes to me,' said Finch, as he examined the remains of the fire. He continued poking and then picked up a sliver of burnt metal from which hung some blackened shards of glass. He held it up on the end of his stick for Morgan to see.

'Didn't you say this fella was wearin' spectacles?' he asked.

Morgan nodded. 'Why did he stop to change his disguise?'

'Because him and his friends ain't headed in a straight line for the border, that's for sure. See where these tracks lead?'

'They're going towards San Marcos. What for, I wonder?'

'San Marcos ain't far away enough from Austin for folks hidin' out after a bank robbery,' said Finch as he got back on his horse. 'My guess is they're headin' for New Braunfels and if we're gonna catch up afore they get there we'll have to move fast.' Then he suddenly set off at a gallop as his employer fell in behind.

Sean and his companions were making slow but steady progress across the Balcones Escarpment, an uneven landscape of limestone covered by a layer of thin soil. The rolling prairie lands of the Texas hill country lay more than thirty miles ahead of them. There the waters of Comal Spring would lead them into the city of New Braunfels. Out here, in this bleak expanse of rock, dust and heat, Sean wished they could reach their destination tonight.

'I reckon we've got about three hours until sunset,' he told the others, glancing up at the sky.

'We'd best keep going until then. There's no telling who might be after us,' warned Chiquita.

'Don't you worry, that fat fool Morgan will still be snoring in his office,' laughed Munro.

They had reached a rise in the escarpment and Pedro pointed to a spot in the distance behind them where two small figures moved rapidly in their direction.

'I wonder who they are,' he said.

'A lot of people travel this way so it's probably nothing to worry about,' said Sean. 'Still, we'd better keep our distance, just in case.'

They moved on, heading south west

while the sun hung above them like an angry yellow eye and its scorching heat sapped their strength. Far behind, Morgan stopped and took a swig from his canteen before mopping his brow with a large handkerchief. He winced as his companion spat out a long black stream of fluid on the ground. He regarded the chewing of tobacco as a filthy habit but said nothing. After all, Finch had not been hired for his social graces.

'Do you see them yet?' he asked.

'Yeah, they're up yonder. We'd better hang back a little.'

'Why? I want that money and those land deeds back as soon as possible!' insisted the banker.

'Sure you do,' responded Finch calmly. 'A surprise attack is the best way so we don't wanna be catchin' up with them folks before nightfall.'

Morgan nodded reluctantly. 'Use your own methods. Just make sure you get results.'

Finch did not reply. He was thinking about the land deeds Morgan had mentioned. The contents of that deposit box must be very valuable indeed. Why else would the banker be willing to pay so much for their safe return? He stole a surreptitious glance at his sweating companion and felt a stab of envy. Finch was the man who took all the risks, who did others' dirty work for them but the rewards always seemed paltry compared to those enjoyed by his rich paymasters. Slowly, an alternative plan began to form in his mind, one that would leave him wealthier than he had ever dreamed of being.

The afternoon slowly blended into dusk and the air grew cooler. Sean found a sheltered spot and they made camp for the night beneath an overhanging ledge of rock. After a supper of bacon, biscuits and beans, Pedro took the first watch and settled down by the fire while the others slept.

Finch crawled on his belly towards the lone figure on guard, making barely a sound. Morgan crouched behind, watching nervously as his hired killer moved in closer. The bounty hunter felt the rock in his hand and slowly rose up behind the unsuspecting Pedro. The Mexican half turned as he sensed a movement behind him at the last moment but it was too late. The rock struck the back of his head before he could cry out and he slumped against his assailant who lowered him gently to the ground.

Finch now drew out a pair of pistols and stood by the flickering firelight before the three sleeping figures. 'I'll stand guard here if you want to look for your property, Mr Morgan,' he told the banker. 'I suggest you let their horses go if you find it.'

Morgan went rummaging and a few minutes later, Sean and his companions were awoken by the sound of galloping hoofs.

'Keep still, all of you. I don't aim to shoot unless I have to.' Finch's voice sounded loud in the nocturnal silence and not one of his prisoners dared move.

'Who are you and what do you want?' demanded Sean.

'My name's not important, but if you don't have what I want you'll end the night beggin' to tell me where it is,' Finch told him.

Then Morgan approached carrying the leather bag. 'It's all here, everything. You don't have to waste any time,' he told the bounty hunter excitedly.

Finch nodded. 'Good, Mr Morgan. Would you be kind enough to collect their guns for me?' he asked.

The banker moved quickly among them, took their gunbelts and stuffed them into the leather bag before returning to Finch's side.

'If you'd like to put that on my horse, Mr Morgan, I'd be happy to carry it for you,' said the bounty hunter.

'Don't kill them until I get back, Finch. I want to see you do it.'

'Sure, there's no hurry.'

'That's the one who robbed me!' shouted Morgan, when he came back, pointing at Munro.

'That was a neat job you pulled,' said Finch with genuine admiration. Then his eyes narrowed. 'Say, don't I know you from someplace?'

Munro did not reply and then Finch spoke again. 'I got it. You're George Munro. You're lucky I got bigger things in store or else I'd turn you in.'

'I know you too, a bounty hunter who always caught the man you were after but never brought any of them back alive,' said Munro, evenly.

'I always figured it was less trouble that way,' replied Finch, as he spat out some chewed tobacco.

'You can quit talking now and get on with what I'm paying you for,' Morgan cut in, impatiently.

'I don't aim to shoot these folks,' said Finch without looking at him.

'Then I'll damn well do it myself!'

The banker's gun was barely out of its holster before Finch shot him straight through the heart. Morgan crumpled to the ground and the bounty hunter kicked the dead man's gun away into the wilderness. The others stared at their captor in silence, wondering what would happen next.

10

There was a long pause before anyone dared speak. 'Let me guess what happened,' said Munro at length. 'Morgan hired you to track and kill us but then you figured what we stole was worth a lot more than he was paying you.'

'That's about the size of it. Well, I'll let you folks get some rest seein' as you got a long walk ahead of you.'

'All our supplies were on those horses. How are we supposed to make it to New Braunfels in tomorrow's heat without food or water?' demanded Sean. 'You might as well just shoot us.'

'I reckon it's more fun this way,' said Finch, as he backed away from them towards his horse. Then he disappeared into the darkness and the sound of galloping hoofs faded away into the night.

There was a groan from nearby as

Pedro recovered consciousness. Chiquita threw her blanket aside and went over to him as he tried to sit up.

'What happened?' he asked her, as he felt the egg-shaped bump on the back of his head.

She briefly explained while tearing a strip from the bottom of her blouse to make a bandage.

'I'm sorry. If I'd been more alert this never would have happened,' he told them.

'It was nobody's fault. We got caught unawares and that's that. The question is: what are we going to do about it?' asked Sean.

'Things aren't as bad as they seem,' said Munro. 'There are springs along the escarpment if you know where to look. I reckon we could make it to New Braunfels on foot if we leave early before it gets too hot.'

'Finch didn't seem to think so,' said Sean gloomily.

'Finch worked out in Arizona and New Mexico but he doesn't know this territory as well as me. There's water, all right, in the springs that feed the San Marcos River and two that I know of between here and New Braunfels.'

'Then I guess we'd better try to get some rest,' said Sean with a sigh of resignation.

Sleep did not come easily to any of them, however, and it was a weary group of travellers who set off in the dawn light. Pedro still had his gun on him and they also stumbled across the one which had belonged to the unfortunate Morgan so they at least had some protection from bandits. Chiquita's canteen had been beside her as she slept so they also had a little water. Nevertheless, it was noon by the time they reached the first spring, by which time they had all developed a raging thirst.

The four of them lay at the edge of the water gulping it in greedily. Suddenly, a shadow passed across the sun and they were greeted by a familiar voice:

'Howdy. I bet you folks weren't expecting to see me out here.'

Sean turned in surprise and looked up into Clancy's battle-scarred features. 'Howdy, Clancy,' was all he could think of to say in return. He was even more surprised when the deserter held up the leather case Finch had stolen from them the previous night.

'I guess this belongs to you, but I told the boys we'd deduct a fee for our trouble. I hope you don't mind but a man has to eat.' Clancy tossed the bag over while holding up a generous wad of cash containing several thousand dollars.

'I don't mind at all but how did you get it?' a nonplussed Sean asked him.

Clancy grinned and tapped the side of his broken nose. 'Here, I'll show you.'

The four followed him along a short path which led to a cave. Several of the Mexicans who had previously followed Chavez were standing around outside and Sean noticed that the horses stampeded by Morgan had been rounded up.

'After Chavez grabbed Quinn and you left to follow them, we all decided to team up. We were on our way to

Mexico when we came across the horses.' Clancy gestured for them to follow him into the cave. 'Let me show you what we found next.'

Inside, Finch sat bound and huddled up against the limestone wall. He had clearly been beaten and two men stood guard over him.

'It seems our friend here don't like Mexicans too much. We sent Francisco out foragin' for some game, thought he might find a jack-rabbit for the pot but he ran into this fella instead.' Clancy then grabbed a fistful of Finch's hair and jerked the man's head back sharply. 'But we caught you, didn't we? Only it was too late for Francisco after you'd cut out his innards while the poor bastard was still alive!'

No response came from Finch's swollen lips and Clancy gave him another punch before letting the prisoner's head slump forward on to his chest.

'After we searched him, I guessed from the land deeds it was stuff you'd been after. It took a while to get the truth out of him about what happened and then we just waited for you to show up.'

Clancy then handed them their guns back before drawing out his pistol. 'Well, I guess there's no sense in keepin' this polecat alive any longer — '

'No!' cried Sean. 'Let us take him back to San Tomas with us. He'll get justice all right, but once he's had a fair trial.'

The deserter frowned. 'Are you sure about that? He's meaner than a whole pit full o' rattlesnakes and could give you some trouble along the way.'

'We won't be taking any chances with him, Clancy, but that's how I want it.' Sean looked at the others for their approval and they all nodded.

Clancy shrugged. 'You must be crazy, but have it your own way.'

Chiquita stepped forward and kissed the deserter on the cheek. 'That's just to say thank you on behalf of the people of San Tomas,' she told him.

Clancy beamed in response. 'I guess

I'll have to start doin' more good deeds from now on,' he told her.

As they mounted their horses to leave, Sean turned to Munro. 'I reckon this is where we part company. We've got what we came for and it's safer for you to stick with Clancy from now on. Avoid the main towns and get yourself over the border as soon as you can.'

'You're letting me go? I can't believe that Marshal Sean Barry would really allow an escaped convict to go free.'

'You once told me that there comes an evil day in every man's life when he has to stand up for what's right and fight wickedness but there also comes a merciful day, a time to let bygones be bygones. You've changed, Munro, atoned for the past and I don't see any sense in sending you back to prison now.'

'I think Sean's right,' added Chiquita. 'You'll do more good as a free man.'

Pedro extended his hand to shake. 'Good luck, *amigo*. You've earned a second chance.'

Munro grasped Pedro's hand and

said farewell to each of them in turn. 'I'm sorry I deceived you all at first by pretending to be my brother, but if I hadn't I'd still be the man I was before.'

'Well, if you want, when you get down to Mexico you can spend the rest of your life in a monastery. How's that sound?' said Sean.

Munro laughed. 'No, I think I'll find myself a wife and settle down with a cantina or a small ranch. I've never tried my hand at an honest living and I can't wait to find out what it's like.'

'What about you, Clancy? What will you do?'

The deserter shrugged as he bound the barely conscious Finch on to his horse. 'I'll make out somehow. At least I've got enough cash to make a fresh start.' Then he slapped the horse's rump and held up a large hand in farewell. 'Y'all stay careful now,' he said as he waved them off.

They tried to maintain a steady pace as they made their way across rough ground under the harsh glare of sunlight.

They had lost several hours by travelling on foot that morning and would now be lucky to reach their destination by nightfall. Finch slumped low in the saddle but gradually recovered from the beating he had received. He made no attempt to persuade them to let him go, however, and said nothing, his gaze focused on the leather bag which now hung from Sean's saddle.

They stopped briefly for a rest and Chiquita tended their prisoner's cuts and bruises. She asked him what grudge he had against Americans of Mexican origin.

'I got nothin' against Mexicans as long as they stay in Mexico and leave Texas for the Texans,' he told her.

'I was born and raised here, it is my country too,' she replied defiantly.

'There's no point arguing with the likes of him,' said Pedro in disgust. 'He'd still be keeping slaves if he could.'

Finch's battered features contorted into a sly grin. 'Yeah, I'd keep them in their place too.'

'All right, that's enough. We don't want to hear that kind of talk,' said Sean.

'Gimme a piece of tobacco to chew and I won't say another word,' replied the bounty hunter. 'There's some in my saddle-bag.'

Sean tore off a piece and shoved it into the prisoner's hands, which were bound in front of him as he sat resting on a rock. Finch put it into his mouth and chewed on it thoughtfully, watching and waiting as he did so. Perhaps if he was clever enough, he might just be able to regain his freedom.

'I never heard of this San Tomas you're takin' me to. Where is it?' asked Finch.

'It's a couple of days' ride from San Antonio,' replied Sean.

'I can't ride that far. Them Mexicans beat me up pretty bad and I gotta bad leg.'

'We'll take the stage from New Braunfels to San Antonio. You should be able to make it that far.'

Finch was silent for a moment. 'Say, don't you figure on bein' some kinda lawman?'

'I'm a marshal.'

'Well, marshals ain't supposed to rob from banks or let thieves like Munro go free. If you put me on trial, there's a lot I could say that might get you into a heap o' trouble.'

Sean shrugged. 'I'm sure you must know what kind of a crook Morgan was. He helped his friend to buy land with money stolen from the people of San Tomas. When that comes out, we won't face any charges over taking it back.'

'You still had Munro and let him go,' insisted Finch.

It was Chiquita who answered him this time. 'Oh you mean the priest, Fr Joseph Munro. That's who everyone in San Tomas thought he was. If you're looking for George Munro, there's a headstone in the churchyard with that name on it.'

'Munro had a twin brother,' added

Pedro by way of explanation. 'Who can say for certain which one is which?'

'I let you go, didn't I? Morgan would have shot you all if I hadn't stopped him,' Finch reminded them.

'You left us with no horses, food, water or guns. I'd hardly call that letting us go,' snorted Sean derisively. 'You'll get what's coming to you and that's that.'

The bounty hunter lapsed once more into a sullen silence as he worked at loosening the bonds on his wrists. Had he been released, Finch might have ridden away without further trouble but his captors had now used up their chances. He would find a way to kill all three of them because the contents of that leather bag were never going to reach San Tomas, not if Blake Finch could help it.

They trudged on through the heat of the afternoon, Finch lagging behind slightly as the rope frayed with continued rubbing against the pommel of his saddle. Finally, he managed to work his hands free and allowed his horse to draw almost level with Pedro's. Sean and Chiquita were further ahead, engrossed in conversation. Finch moved swiftly but silently, whipping the pistol from Pedro's holster before the Mexican was aware of what had happened. The muzzle was pressed hard against Pedro's ribs and he froze, raising his hands as his horse stopped.

'Stop right there, you two, or your friend's a dead man!' Finch called out.

Sean and Chiquita drew to a halt and the bounty hunter told them to turn around very slowly. 'One false move and I'll blow Pedro inside out,' he added grimly.

They had no choice other than to obey and when they were facing him, Finch ordered them to dismount and step away from their horses. Then they both stood, hands in the air, waiting tensely.

'Now, take off those gunbelts and throw 'em away from you.' Chiquita undid hers and dropped it on the ground. Sean hesitated.

'Come on, what are you waitin' for?'

demanded Finch.

'Once I'm unarmed, there's nothing to stop you killing all three of us.'

Finch shook his head. 'Do as I say and you can go, same as last time except I'll leave you with supplies, but if you don't throw that gunbelt down, Pedro gets it.'

Sean shook his head as he met his adversary's blank gaze. 'No, you won't shoot him as long as I've got a gun because then you'd have nothing left to bargain with. I can draw faster than you could kill us both.'

'You won't draw that gun, though, because you know I'll kill Pedro if you do.'

'If I figure that you plan on killing us all anyway, what difference does it make? I might as well trade his life for mine and Chiquita's.'

'You're right, Sean. I'm a dead man anyway. Save yourself and Chiquita!' Pedro urged him.

'You shut up!' cried Finch, ramming the gun into his hostage's ribs so that

Pedro cried out in pain. This was not turning out the way he had expected. His bluff had been called and he was unsure of what to do next.

'Drop that gunbelt now or I'll shoot!' shouted the bounty hunter in desperation.

Sean shook his head calmly. 'Look, Finch. Why don't you just back away slowly? I won't go for my gun as long as you don't fire yours. That way, everyone gets out of here alive, including you.'

There was a pause while Finch turned this offer over in his mind. The marshal was a cool customer and smarter than he had expected.

'All right, but I want the money.' He looked hard at Chiquita. 'Get that leather bag and come over here with it, real slow.'

'Do as he says,' added Sean. 'I'm not willing to risk our lives over it.'

Chiquita brought the bag over and Finch ordered her to hook it over his saddle. He did not move his gun an inch or take his eyes off Sean the whole time. Then he backed his horse away from them, holding the reins in one hand and Pedro's pistol in the other. The others stood silent and still, as if cast in brass.

Then the sound of a gunshot echoed all around them. Finch's horse reared and he threw his arms up before falling from the saddle to land face down on the ground. The bullet had hit him between the shoulders and Sean stepped forward to turn the body over. Finch's sightless eyes stared up at the sky with the same blank expression they had held when he was alive. Chiquita shivered as Sean prised the gun from the dead man's fingers and handed it back to Pedro.

In the distance, a lone figure on horseback held up a rifle and waved in farewell. Munro had obviously decided to track them until he knew they were safe, no doubt at Clancy's suggestion. They waved back and the former bank robber disappeared over the horizon.

Sean turned back to Chiquita. 'We'd better hurry if we're going to reach

New Braunfels before dark. I want to be on that stage in the morning so we can reach San Antonio as soon as possible.'

'Why are you so keen to get to San Antonio all of a sudden?' she asked him.

'Because that's where we're going to get married,' he told her, as he slipped his arms around her waist.

The long kiss which followed was interrupted by Pedro. 'When the honeymoon's over, I know a little town that needs a good sheriff.'

'What do you say?' Chiquita asked him, breathlessly.

'Well, I guess it's better than robbing another bank!'

Then all three of them laughed as they threw the wads of cash from the leather bag up in the air with delight.

THE END